Booth's Sister

**Center Point
Large Print**

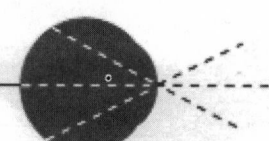

**This Large Print Book carries the
Seal of Approval of N.A.V.H.**

Booth's Sister

Jane Singer

CENTER POINT PUBLISHING
THORNDIKE, MAINE

This Center Point Large Print edition
is published in the year 2009 by arrangement with
BelleBooks, Inc.

The text of this Large Print edition is unabridged.
In other aspects, this book may vary
from the original edition.
Printed in the United States of America.
Set in 16-point Times New Roman type.

ISBN: 978-1-60285-516-8

Library of Congress Cataloging-in-Publication Data

Singer, Jane, 1947-
  Booth's sister / Jane Singer. -- Large print ed.
    p. cm.
  Originally published: Smyrna, Ga. : Bell Bridge Books, c2008.
  ISBN 978-1-60285-516-8 (library binding : alk. paper)
 1. Clarke, Asia Booth, 1835-1888--Fiction. 2. Booth, John Wilkes, 1838-1865--Fiction.
   3. Lincoln, Abraham, 1809-1865--Assassination--Fiction. 4. Large type books.
   I. Title.

PS3619.I57235B66 2009
813'.6--dc22

2009009289

For my parents, Morton and Frances Singer

Time tames the loss.
Memory and all love are eternal.

Author's Introduction

I had seen only two photos of her. They were tattered, very old and riveting. She was a beauty—black-eyed and fine boned—her soul-weary gaze unchanged from the intense young woman trapped on a lonely farm to a solemn matron enduring a forced exile in England. Her name was Asia Booth, the beloved sister, teacher and other self of a famous young actor who changed history with a single gunshot.

On the moonless night of April 14, 1865, days after a plot to blow up the White House failed, John Wilkes Booth killed President Abraham Lincoln. During the twelve days of his flight through the Southern Maryland outback, Asia Booth was arrested and held in the Philadelphia home she shared with her husband. On April 26, after a massive manhunt, Booth was cornered and killed in a burning barn in Port Royal, Virginia.

Had her brother lived to face a trial, Asia surely would have been charged, for Booth used her home as a safe house, taught her the Confederate cipher code and entrusted her with papers revealing names and most likely, plots for the destruction of the United States government.

"A desperate turn towards evil had come," she wrote, after hearing her brother damn the United States and the "falsely" elected president. It was her memoir called The Unlocked Book—a paean to a lost boy penned in secret during the last years of her life and smuggled to a trusted friend—that moved me.

I needed to know more.

My daughter Jessica, who has, with humor and grace, long endured my passion to ferret out and write about the unknown men and women in the Civil War, traveled with me to the Booth family home in Bel Air, Maryland, several years ago. For years I'd been researching the Lincoln assassination, was writing a non-fiction work about terrorism in the Civil War and, for good measure, completing a lengthy trek through Southern Maryland on the trail of Lincoln's assassin. Our first stop was at the Surratt House Museum in Clinton, Maryland; an extraordinary repository for all things related to the Lincoln tragedy. The ready scholars on hand were and are invaluable resources and friends.

On we went.

"Not another farmhouse with spiders and people in costume who speak from another time," Jessica said, longing for a nice hotel room with thick towels where she could study for a final exam in peace.

"Just one more stop," I said. "It's only a hundred or so miles north of here." My true companion-daughter rolled her eyes and pulled out a map. And soon, well, soon enough, we were bumping along a dirt road; any evidence of the mini-malls and gas stations we passed—a memory—another time away.

"Tudor Hall," is and was the hand-hewn creation of Asia's half-mad tragedian father Junius Brutus Booth—a tattered place rife with tales of ghostly apparitions, little changed in one hundred and sixty years, suspended in time. Asia's feather bed and rocker remain in her small room, her brother's bookcase, bed and nightstand a whisper away, in his.

There was a sadness, a loneliness about the place. But there was also the sure feel of youthful lives, the dips and stutters and strangeness of country kids raised on Shakespeare with mostly each other for company until the Civil War consumed John Booth and sent them both to an unimaginable hell.

We spent the night. A soundless, sweet one for Jessica nestled in Asia's bed. A troubled one for me, sleepless in John Wilkes Booth's room: lights and shadows playing on the walls, plenty of moaning wind brought by a sudden June storm. In the morning, Dorothy and Howard Fox, the gentle and genteel owners of the house smiled tolerantly at me as I wandered in the dewy grass. They puttered about the kitchen and served Jessica a country breakfast she would wax poetic about for years. Just before we left, I lingered in Asia's room. I knew so much about her brother and his deed and almost nothing about her. Feeling just a little silly, I asked her if I might write her story. I asked silently of course. Maybe, the still, June air moved a bit. Maybe there was a small breeze. I left her room, the imagined scent of lilacs lingering in the air. In the narrow, narrow hallway that separated the ill-fated boy and girl, I made a promise. I would tell her story: Not a justification or a supplication, but a tale, a sister's tale. Herein lies a promise kept.

Jane Singer

Your tale . . . would cure deafness.
   The Tempest by William Shakespeare

Prologue

My brother killed Abraham Lincoln. That is my weight, my shame. While he remained at large, I was held captive in my home. I should have told the soldiers who came with guns drawn and bayonets at the ready this true thing: I might have stopped him, for I harbored him and kept his secrets. I was a pie safe locked tight and guilty as he.

When John Wilkes Booth was small and in my stormy keep, I fused us, so alike in face and form, into one muddle of a being. He was beautiful always. I was hat-rack thin with hair like a Hottentot's and a longing to be him as deep and wide as any river I ever did see. "You'll teach him the verses, Asia, and make him the greatest Booth of them all," my father said. "Poor Hamlet weeps and sighs in your head, that I know," he added, forbidding me to ever set foot on a stage.

The memory of the world around us—our celebrated family, the words of Shakespeare as necessary as morning porridge, our reckless, enchanted childhood deep in the woods—was a symphony of endless variation.

I watched as my brother grew to manhood; a

famous actor with half the country in a lather about him and an easy passage through the world that lay beyond our sorry farm overgrown with tick weed and blighted corn. When war came, though our family remained dead loyal to Mr. Lincoln's Union, my brother did not. He was a Rebel to his bones and no ordinary soldier. John Wilkes Booth was an enemy agent on an enemy mission. And I who lived in him, lived *for* him could not, would not turn away.

On April 15, 1865, the day the President died, rain poured incessantly as though ordered by a raging god to drown we sinners in our sleep.

I begin my tale with that raw April dawn. I begin with rain.

. . . So full of dismal terror was the time.
Richard III by William Shakespeare

1

Philadelphia
April 15, 1865

The gentle thrum of rain was soothing. I lay abed in my husband's house, a new life nesting in me. I traced the outline of the tiny body as it twitched and bumped and tickled. My first child would soon slumber in a grand nursery under a picture of his uncle, Johnny Booth.

"Remember me in your prayers," my brother wrote on the photo we hung—the bold, snapping black-eyed broth of him—just over the crib. Dithering, vaporous women wept at the sight of John Booth, tearing off bits of his clothes as keepsakes as though cloth were flesh. *Pity them,* I mused. Pity the lasses that long for a famous man bright and beautiful as a new moon . . .

"Christ, oh, Christ!" My husband's cry jolted me from my reverie.

He was hopping from one foot to the other pulling at his pants in a frenzied effort to get them closed; wobbling and rubber-kneed in a minstrel's dance that was no dance at all. "God help me," he whispered.

He hurled the morning newspaper on the floor. I struggled to my feet, my sleeping gown slipping from my shoulders, the hem caught around my ankles. I stumbled after him into the hallway. He'd forgotten his boots, racing away in stocking feet as though fleeing a fire.

"Answer me!" There was only silence save the slamming of doors.

"Gillie?" I whispered at the door of my trusted friend and companion. Her bed was empty.

I moved further down the hall. "Mama?" Just then I remembered my mother had gone to stay with friends in New York. And, it was cook's day off.

Perhaps someone summoned my husband to tell him his precious theatre had burned in the night. Or had disaster befallen the sloe-eyed actress who stroked his hand with uncommon tenderness and thought I did not notice? I was meant to be such a woman, to have light, long fingers, their tips scented with lavender, paid to float onstage to wild applause. My husband was passing happy once with me. Sometimes we'd dance till dawn, a waltz or a horn piper's jig weightless as leprechauns floating through a cloud. But the war and my brother's rebel stand had winnowed him to a shadow I barely knew.

I swore my tiny child rocked in my belly as if to cheer me, as if to say, "Wait for me, for the new-struck eyes of me. Wait for love."

I walked toward my room, made heady by visions of the child and the flash of freedom at my husband's departure. I'd don britches and boots and ride far from this place, past the city into the woods. I'd not return 'til midnight passed, praying my brother's messengers would not land on my porch like nighthawks with more ciphers to decode: Men I met in shadow and prayed never to see again, the armed Rebels ordered to make themselves known to no one but me. Because my husband returned at all hours and slept like the dead 'til dawn, they passed in safety and silence.

And always, as I handed off the dispatches because I could not refuse my brother, I wished us young again, with nothing more pressing than reciting a verse of Shakespeare's at the tip of dawn. *Trip away,* I'd whisper to him, *make no stay; meet me all by break of day.* Tousled and hungry we'd drift through the silent house to the kitchen where yellow-topped johnnycakes shimmered like buttercups in Gillian's iron skillet.

In that empty hallway, I ached for that lost time and sang quietly to myself: *When that I was and a little bitty boy, with a hey, ho the wind and the rain. A foolish thing is but a toy, for the rain, it raineth . . .*

Someone grabbed me by the hair and clapped a hand over my mouth. Hard against my back I felt the body of a man. He yanked me across the landing, my legs bouncing like a rag doll. "Don't make a sound," he whispered, his mouth against my ear.

Soldiers with weapons drawn moved silently up the stairs toward us. I struggled against him. "God damn it, don't move," he said.

One of the men had Gillian. She reached for me and broke free.

"Shoot the nigger if she takes another step," my captor ordered. The bravest woman I had ever known stood down, though her body fairly vibrated—the fix of her green eyes set deep in a fine-cut ebony face and long, strong legs put me in mind of a wildcat caught mid-spring.

Soldiers were all around us now, opening doors, wardrobes, moving through the entryway toward the parlor, flattening themselves against the walls.

"Captain!"

"Anything?" My attacker demanded.

"No, sir, just her and the nigger."

"Outside?"

"We've secured, sir."

"Every inch, every God damn inch?"

"We have, sir."

He pulled me into the bedroom. I spotted the paper my husband had thrown to the floor. Hard black lines tracked across the page.

Lincoln Shot at Ford's Theatre!
Actor Booth Sought!

I broke from his grasp and stumbled to the staircase, clutching the arm of the banister. A window exploded above me. I fell to the carpet, my arms over my head as pieces of glass landed on my back and hands. Blood streamed from somewhere on my body. I struggled to rise.

"Stay down," he ordered and pushed me hard to the floor. There were gunshots. Sharp loud bursts. And voices, loud and louder still.

"Hang them all!"

"God damn the devil Booths!"

"Burn the house!"

He yanked me to my feet, twisting my arm behind my back. Only then did I realize that I was not badly hurt; that the blood was coming from a cut on my hand. He ignored this, his face so close to mine I could feel the hiss that was his breathing.

Gillian rushed to my side.

"Don't you grab her like that, she's gonna have a baby!" She wrapped her apron around my wound, all the while railing at the men, "I'll see you in hell if you hurt her!"

"She's got a rolling pin under there, Captain. That is one killer nigger," a soldier said, wrestling the rough wooden implement from Gillian's hand. "I got a pistol from off her boot before."

Bravo, my love, I thought. I turned to face to my captor, saw a short, red beard, a worn, young face and hard, gray eyes. His hands were huge and black-gloved. I was thrust into a chair.

"Where is Booth?" He stood over me, his belt at the level of my eyes.

"I don't know."

"And your husband?"

I didn't answer.

"She don't know beans about shit, Captain Martin," another said. The red beard had a name.

"Name?" Martin demanded.

"Asia."

"Your whole name!"

"Clarke. Asia Booth Clarke."

"Where is he?"

"Who?"

"Your brother."

"Which brother?"

"Don't game me, woman."

"I have three brothers."

"John Wilkes Booth!" he said, as though mouthing a curse.

"I swear, I don't know."

"Lock them in," Martin ordered.

A mob was forming in the street. Through the shattered window I saw and heard them: Men with brickbats and pistols cursing and firing at the house and a cordon of soldiers keeping them back. I heard the keening of a woman: A high, long wail.

They tied us to the bedpost and left the room. Gillian's hands, touching mine, were cold as the grave.

"They got my gun," she whispered.

"Mine is below in the pantry, Gillie."

"We got no defenses now, child."

"Even if, Gillie. We're no match at all." I pressed against her.

"What do they want with us, Asia?"

"The President's been shot."

"Oh, God Jesus, no!" she cried

"The paper said they're looking for Johnny. I don't believe it."

Gillie offered no comfort. She prayed.

"He would never harm the President, Gillie. He only meant to—"

"Don't you say nothing! You got that baby inside you."

"He didn't shoot anyone." I was shaking and gasping for breath. "Maybe he did. God, I can't remember. I couldn't see him—"

"The soldiers are coming back, hush!"

"I have to think, Gillie."

"Don't say nothing!"

The door flew open.

"Get up, woman," Martin commanded as he untied me.

I faked a faint and dropped to the floor. I was bred in the bone to be the actor my brother was. But at the last moment, my head struck the heavy warming iron that sat by the bed. I saw lights— bold and flashing.

"Is she dead?" I heard Martin ask through a fog

in my head. "I can't interrogate a person who isn't breathing."

I felt his hand on my heart, his mouth close to mine.

"Shake the woman, for Christ's sake," he ordered.

"Don't touch her again." The hard voice was Gillian's.

"Quiet, Mammy," someone said, "or we'll blow your head off."

There was a rushing in my brain. And darkness.

"Find a doctor," I heard Martin say.

I felt Gillian's hand stroking my face, her lips against my temple. I struggled to open my eyes, to move, but could not.

"I can't see, Gillie." I was slipping in and out of consciousness.

"The doctor will come, child."

"Where am I?"

"Somewhere in the middle," Gillian said.

"Help me."

"Go away in your mind, Asia."

"Where?"

"Go home."

"How?" I whispered, as it grew darker.

"Remember the breeze we'd make for your papa? 'Cue the wind!' he'd say. And we'd pump those bellows until we was near a faint, remember?"

"Don't leave me."

"Never. Think of wind," she said.

. . . The truth is, she and I—long since con-
tracted—are now so sure that nothing can dissolve
us . . .
> The Merry Wives of Windsor
> by William Shakespeare

2

I saw myself, a girl-child of eleven, racing along
the road astride a bone-white stallion. My quarry
was a small boy, nearly eight, running just ahead. I
was summoning him with Shakespeare's words. *A*
fox when one has caught her and such a daughter
will sure to the slaughter! I reached down and
grabbed a shock of his thick, black hair.

"So the fool follows after," he said, vaulting on
the horse's back, holding tight to my waist.

"Where now, Asia?"

"You'll see." The earth-baked odor of horse
sweat and the little boy at my back was a perfec-
tion of the senses. I gripped the stallion's flanks
between my thighs. No sidesaddle frippery for me.
I rode astride my steed as though I was a man.

We leapt a tall fence, swerving through a spill of
lilac bushes toward the mossy rocks behind the
springhouse. In the cool shadows, I took a bottle of
India ink and a sharp quill from my overalls. I
began my task.

"You're hurting me, Asia!"

21

"Not for long, Johnny, hush." I gripped his hand and pressed it flat. Tiny tears like dragonfly eggs came to his huge, black eyes. "Almost, almost . . . there." I placed his small hand against my larger one. I plunged the stylus into the ink, pressing the point into my skin. "The same, you see?" Just at the base of our thin wrists I scratched the name "Booth" in tiny letters. "Bastard boys are shunned, Johnny, and I am fated to be a woman with no name save my husband's. So I have branded us both."

I took him in my arms. "We shall be Booths forever even if Mama and Father never marry. I'm tired of saying we're the *Timoneys,* daddy's cousins from Galway and I can't remember the shipwreck we survived that supposedly killed our parents anyway."

"Daddy told me that our true mama and papa died from eating bad potatoes," the boy said. "Can you really croak that way?"

"There was a famine, dunderhead. They didn't have any damn potatoes. That's why they died!" I licked away the blood drops raised by the pen from his wrist. "Run, boy. I'll count to ten."

"What comes after ten?" he asked.

"Fourteen."

"Is that what the blind tutor lady said that Father brought because she'd never tell where we lived? She smelled bad."

"You put manure on her chair, Johnny!"

"She said children shouldn't read Shakespeare and sat on our cat. I hated her."

I opened my eyes wide and, staring as one sightless might be, pushed my hand right into my brother's face and grabbed the end of his nose. "Demon's proboscis! Oh, my lord, please send me into next Tuesday. Get me gone surely, Mr. Booth. These are wicked orphans!" I stumbled forward with outstretched arms and banged straight into a tree. "I cannot teach math-em-aticals to this boy and girl!"

"They don't need numbers, missus," Johnny said, intoning low like his father. "Verse shall wake 'em and verse shall put 'em to slumber."

We howled with laughter at the memory of our one-and-only teacher, who prayed for a tornado to blow her to the next county.

"Catch the cat!" My brother raced away.

"I see you, Johnny Booth," I said, crawling between the legs of my steed into thick Oleander bushes—white devil flowers sodden with dew. "Who is a true Booth to his bones? Now the roof."

I grabbed him and pulled him to his feet. He followed me up the giant cherry tree to the top of the house—to the tin roof boiling in the sun.

"I'm afraid, Asia," he yelled, hopping up and down like a baby robin that felt a fire on his feet.

"Jump, Johnny, or else you'll incinerate!"

"Will you catch me, Asia?"

"Always!"

Clutching strong branches, we swung high in the air as red fruit rained down on the rhyming balcony. From that place, we recited Shakespeare and snippets of Byron and Blake, loud and long so our father might hear us in faraway San Francisco and be proud.

We landed on the ground at the feet of Gillian. She was glowering at us, holding out a letter. "If your heads ain't broke, you all got something from your papa."

"Read it to us, Gillie," I said, feeling my brother's arms and legs for broken bones, my own hands scratched and filthy.

She was bursting proud of her reading and, as she spoke, Johnny and I grinned through the dust and sweat on our faces. A letter from our father was an occasion of bliss as his absences leeched joy from us and made Mama silent as a cottage wren. Gillian read slowly.

My loves,

Whales sing in summer here. The city and even the saloons are filled with gold. People listen to the whales from houses like nests that rock in the wind. I would like to send a ship to float you straight to my arms, but alas, I cannot. When I return, look in my 'sometimes' pocket.

Inside you will see a wooden bear, the most fearsome of all California denizens and surely a beast to be faced down. Of course, when chancing upon him near a mining camp in Sacramento, I lulled him with a sonnet. Whereupon, a great gold tear came to his one eye, so moved was he by my performance, or perhaps he'd eaten his fill of miner's gold and it oozed from his solitary duct.

Tell your beloved Mama to kiss you many times for me. And remind Gillian that she is noble and proper royalty.

Your pater in all matters of love,
Junius Brutus Booth.

"That's Mr. Junius, alright," Gillie said "Honey words and a glad, good heart. Go on home now, before I give you both a thrashing."

We followed her, clutching Father's letter, reading it over and over. "Maybe he's back already," I said.

"I hope he is, and I hope he's not," Gillian said. "Maybe he brought the gold with him—something to keep this place going. And when he does, we best pray that bear isn't on a leash behind him."

He did not come back so soon. This was not uncommon. We waited and stocked the larder with pippin apples, potatoes, turnips and gooseberry jam and, of course, many bottles of his precious honey wine. We had ceremonies to welcome him home but also a *leaving* ceremony, each and every time he went away.

"How long will you be gone this time, Daddy?" I'd ask.

"When you have carved the pumpkins," he said, "and given them each the glower of poor King Richard shrunk and bent with hating, or when you've seared a luscious smile into the face of the merriest wife of Windsor, then, I shall be home."

We'd dive at him, knocking him to the floor. "Don't go at all, Daddy!"

"And deprive my audiences of my magnificent tragedies? Fame is a harlot. She smothers me with her perfumes and woos me to come to her, uh, cave."

We'd watch as father ambled down the road, his travel bag banging against his back, and tried to picture a creature with dusky, fragrant places that no man could resist.

"Like a circus?" asked Johnny Booth, after I first described this errant woman to him, this creature who lured Father far from us.

"A *Circe*, a *Lorelei*, or somebody dangerous. That's who's got him surely."

We always cried when he left, and were afraid.

I must needs tell thee all . . .
The Merchant of Venice
by William Shakespeare

3

I saw the pumpkins on the fence, some topped with Father's old wigs: tendrils of stark white against crumpled rinds, others with quartz eyes rolled high up in battered heads. I counted the pumpkins. It was one year later. I was eleven.

The smells of brandy and cigars drifted through the air. I followed the odors into the parlor. William Shakespeare's pursed, smug face with its uncommon berry-shaped nose gazed from Father's prized oil that hung over the fireplace. Father's likeness took up nearly the opposite wall in full, king's-gold regalia and velvet, as the sad, lost Hamlet he was, winking or glowering, depending on the light.

Books were stuffed under chairs and tables: Thick, embossed leather tomes brimming with ancient languages, maps of lost rivers, planets and anatomy. Cicada skins pressed into parchment poked from volumes of Byron, Shelley, Blake and their glorious rhymes. And of course, there was every word the Bard ever wrote; bound scripts and books upon books by him and about him were piled high as a man's head.

We read while we ate. Meals were silent as we rested our foreheads on dusty pages, spooning food into the corners of our mouths, so as not to deface one precious word.

"Prince Hal's name is missing an 'L' on page 432 where a female urchin drooled blackberry!" Father yelled. "How abominable. He is now Prince 'Ha!' "

"Sorry, Dad," I said, trying to lick the stain from the page.

"Just read, don't eat then!" he said. I swallowed the rest of my pie, wiping my mouth with part of the tablecloth. After the meal, Father toasted his homecoming—twice.

I buried my face in his coat that smelled of paint and powder; hard and close to see if there was any wind left in it. I reached deep into the coat. "Is that a real gold nugget in your 'sometimes pocket,' Daddy?"

"What do you think, Asia? Hacked and mined by goat men with beards to their knees, was it?" he said, holding up a glittering stone.

I spat on my supposed nugget and rubbed it hard. "It's only a rock, Daddy, all the shine washed away."

"Who's the fool now, hasty miss?"

"I'll make something of it!" I said.

With paint and bits of fairy glitter from Father's makeup trunk, the rock took on the sheen of Midas' treasure. "I'm beginning my alchemy. First the fool's rock," I announced. "I'll make gold from bee's nectar, or diamonds from icicles that will never melt." I grabbed my brother by the collar. "Or, make a dazzle of *you*." He tried to pull away. "I will, Johnny, or die trying."

"Let the boy go, Asia," Father said. "Though your intentions are noble."

Gillian swatted me on the behind. "Make something of him later, Asia. Your papa has an announcement."

"Thank you, Queen Anne," Father beamed at her. "I have a surprise for you, my loves. But first, a toast to my new wife." He fell to his knees at my swoony, silky Mama's feet.

"Your wife? Mama is your wife now?" I could hardly believe what I'd heard.

"When I first saw her," Father said, holding Mama close, "she looked like a fresh peony. My Maryanne was not an actress; perish the thought. Just outside the theatre, I bought all her nosegays of violets. Her beauty brought me to my knees."

Johnny and I knew this speech by heart. We recited it along with Father.

"So I whisked her to America," we all intoned. "I will adore her forever." Father grabbed Johnny's hand and mine, placing them on his chest. "On my heart, now! Repeat after me: I will never, ever again speak of Junius Brutus Booth's first wife. She is my spouse no more. Swear!"

"You mean Adelaide, who wheezes when she laughs and has the big behind of a dray horse?" said Johnny Booth, who'd never seen her.

"The woman with bright red locks and a smile as big as Baltimore, you mean," I said, pitying his abandoned English wife and hating her in the same breath.

"Good as dead," Father answered. "Dead as a trivet, or a doorstop, or—"

"You got a divorce?" I asked as my father for good measure, moved our hands up and down across his chest in the pattern of a large cross.

He scowled. "Swear to never speak of her."

"We swear, Dad."

"The good woman gave me a divorce at last, bless her soul. The Timoneys are dead, long live the Booths!" He pulled my brother and me into his arms.

Mama fairly screamed with joy. "Father married me today!" She kissed him again and again.

"What happened to the Timoneys this time, Dad?" I asked from under his coat.

He heaved a great sigh. "Your poor parents died of cholera, or, or the pox, or something, so I shall legally adopt you."

"Except *we're* your real children!" I yelled.

"Yes, Miss Snipp, of course you are. The tale is for visitors, so ye shan't be shunned in the village."

"They don't go to the village," said Gillian.

"They don't go anywhere," I muttered.

"I couldn't spell our name anyway," Johnny said. "Mama, was your wedding beautiful? Did he sing to you?"

"He put me on the old pony," Mama said. "She was draped in wildflowers, and we came home. He *was* singing, as I recall. Think of it—I was carried off like the elf queen on the back of a unicorn." Mama twirled on her toes, nearly capsizing herself and all the dinnerware.

"I don't want to ride a weed-covered pony from a wedding—mine, or anyone else's," I said, suddenly released from my bastard status but not a bit relieved, having had the shame too long. "I'll never, never marry. Who'd have me?"

"Someone wonderful, Asia," Mama answered, stroking my hair—what little she could find, as it was tucked up under a sorry straw hat.

"Now I can show this." Johnny Booth thrust his tattooed hand at father.

"My God," Father said, grabbing him by the wrist. He grasped mine as well.

"Asia made me wear shirts clear over my hands, Daddy. And Mama and the girl never saw," my brother said.

"Yes we did," answered Mama and Gillian in unison.

"Don't ever call Gillian 'the girl' again!" I kicked my brother in the shins.

"Damn straight," said Father, boxing his ears.

Mama and Gillian passed a bottle of champagne between them.

"Am I punished, Dad?" My voice was small.

"No, no, no. It is I who must beg your forgiveness, Asia. It took me so long. My God." He picked us both up. That was no small task for him. We were growing tall. "Come, loves." He staggered toward the door. "We'll celebrate your legitimacy."

"I can't breathe, Daddy," said Johnny Booth from under Father's arm.

"I'll walk, thank you. I'll be along," I said. I pulled free of him and went to Mama. " 'Bout damn time, Mrs. Booth."

"We are enchanted, after all," said Mama, her face shining like the sun.

"Lord, God," said Gillian, "*Enchanted*. Is that it?"

Cupid himself would blush to see me thus transformed to a boy.
The Merchant of Venice
by William Shakespeare

4

"Alas, poor Timoneys, alas, alack," Father crowed as he bumped through the forest, slapping tree trunks with a stick. "We shall not mourn ye."

Johnny Booth joined in. *"Thwack, thwack, thwack!"*

I trudged after the new bridegroom and his son.

My brother bounced in his arms, barely avoiding tree limbs that twisted and cracked as they pass. "Stop smacking me in the head, boy," Father shouted, "or I'll pitch you into the pond where the souls of the Timoneys hunker!"

They disappeared into a thicket. I followed at a run.

"He's in his cups in a tree," Johnny Booth announced, looking lost and very young as I arrived, panting, on the scene.

We were just past the blackberry bushes, at a spot by the water where Father made our theatre in the forest. The wooden stage was studded with glass footlights, each holding a tiny candle that burnt long into the night.

"This crystal chandelier was brought directly

from the site of poor Anne Boleyn's last meal," Father announced, clinging to a limb, hoisting a spangled fixture with a rope. He climbed even higher and hung his treasure from the branches. In spite of its royal provenance, the chandelier had lain on the ground for weeks, covered in bird droppings, awaiting his arrival.

"Think of it," he said, his face glowing with sweat and paint. "Poor Queen Anne's head was nearly off when last she glanced at this marvel. Perhaps, the sparkle gave her a whisper of comfort. Or perhaps not," he murmured, teasing a branch with his bulk.

"Daddy, you'll fall!" my brother cried.

"I shan't, my darling. *Eeee Ah!*" He howled like a banshee. We covered our ears and eyes, expecting a mighty thump. "I summon the fairy Evelina, keeper of fancies, to this spot!" He leapt from the tree to the gold braid rug that lay on the grass. He held aloft a box of red phosphorus sticks with sandpaper along the edge. "Sweet lover, come." He lit the candles one by one, summoning a fairy he believed waited on his every whim and served him goblets of honey wine.

"*Cheroo, tick-tock, tick-tock, cheroo, cheroo.* Appear, tiny female with nipples of rubies. Bless my union with my Maryanne and do not be jealous, for you shall always be my dream lover."

We waited, the mist of the phosphorus making us a bit dizzy, though we couldn't smell or taste it.

"Fairy gas," father called it, having sniffed it close more than once.

"Oh, I see her now. Those tiny teats do sparkle so. Oh, oh, oh, let me dream." He passed out flat on the grass with the honey wine of Evelina imagined on his lips. While father smiled and snored in snorts and whistles, each burst of air causing his face to crinkle and puff up, Johnny and I stole to the edge of the pond.

A giant bullfrog lived there. His mottled green head with eyes like striped orbs of Jupiter rose through lily pads. To win his favor, we paid him tributes of pure silver and dragonflies. In return, I swore, the frog would reveal the ways of the universe: how a man shot with a bullet infused with sunlight might fly, and why some creatures are born witless, others wise. He told a little boy and his sister how to chase away the dragons at the window and where to hide when neighbors come.

I'd secreted five silver spoons stolen from our mother's pine trunk under a rock. I lifted them out and dropped them one by one into the water. His maw opened wide as a blacksmith's fist, and his endless black tongue tickled the spoons before they disappeared. When a russet dragonfly chanced by, I trapped it in my hand.

"No! We mustn't harm this creature, even for the secrets of the world, Asia!" my brother cried.

"It's too late, boy." The frog's tongue lashed the dragonfly, plunging it out of sight into his throat.

"Perhaps, Sister, the dragonfly will escape the belly of the frog as Jonah did the whale."

I pondered this and was oddly comforted, for my brother was beautiful and clever and I was none of those things. "No, boy," I said. "The dragonfly is gone to nothing. Nothing!" I splashed my brother in the face.

"What does the frog say, then, Asia?"

"That our lives have been so long a secret, our true selves are covered over."

"Like snakes, then?" he asked.

"Yep, ragged, itchy ones who never shed. We're damn fixed to lies. How many times could we be introduced as father's relations just sprouted up like mushrooms in the peat bog? 'Here are the Timoney children,' he said. 'Well behaved after such a long crossing. Not one puke out of them as they spanned the sea from England.' *Bah!*"

"Crap!" the boy said, delighted at his profanity. "Crap!"

"Shut up, Johnny. And us with no proper clothes or real school, or—"

"You're my school, Asia."

"Yeah, and I'll drive you till you're blue, now that he can call you a Booth."

"What about Edwin and Junius?" he asked, meaning our older brothers, long out of the house.

"Edwin and Junius Timoney will do as they wish," I said, bitter at their negligence, envious of their free lives. "If they want the name, it's theirs for the picking. We never see them anyway. It's just you now, John Wilkes Booth."

"Let's drown ourselves then," he said brightly, leaning toward the water.

At once, the frog sounded a mighty croak that near blasted us.

"Listen, Johnny. It's a code. Don't you hear him? Two croaks, there, yes. And more. I have it! 'You two must remain on this earth for a very long time,' he said. 'And I will always be here to give you wisdom if you are afraid.'"

I held my brother close. "I'll protect you, always. I love you more than anybody."

"And if Father hates my verses? If I stink like rotted eggs?"

"I'll be there. Or I'll be an actor, too, and go on the stage instead of you."

"You can't," he said, puffed up with knowing. "Ever."

"Stop talking! Or I'll drown you myself."

I had brought my little guitar with us. I thought to smash it on a rock. I felt like screaming. Instead, I shouted a song to the damn frog and anyone or anything that was about. *"Somebody's needing redemption, somebody's heart is a-breaking, somebody's heart is a-breaking, down at the Mad Dog saloon."*

The frog slithered beneath the water. *"Creep and a crawl through the darkness, make me a place at the table, I'm eating the flesh of forgiveness down at the Mad Dog saloon."*

I made a monster face at my brother.

"What's a saloon?" he asked calmly, making his tongue curl and his eyes pop.

"A place where they skin animals and people, dunce boy. You must never go to one. I know these things."

The frog cast a last look back at me as if to say, "Well done. Just keep paying me."

"HELLLP!" I screamed, tossing another silver spoon at the frog.

Gillie came through the trees at a run, brandishing her rolling pin. I grabbed up the remaining spoons and shoved them in the dirt. "Who's dying out here?"

"Nobody, Gillie."

She raised the rolling pin and came straight at me. Johnny Booth jumped on her back. They spun and spun and fell breathless to the ground.

"Don't scream again," she warned me, sitting on my brother's back, "or I'll crack your head."

"Will her brains spill out?" asked Johnny Booth.

"Your thieving ways are gonna be the death of me," Gillian said. "I saw the spoons. What else have you stole?"

"Wisdom," I said.

"Bad, bad child," She glared hard at me. "What about you, King Johnny?" She yanked him to his feet.

"I'm not sure," he answered, yelping at the pinch I gave him.

"That's bunkum and you know it. You thieved from your mama plain and simple."

"We got knowledge!" I yelled, dodging her raised hand.

"You ought to get hard time in the calaboose." She looked around, a sly smile on her face. "By the way, God-awful young things, he's fixing to find you."

I heard my father's voice. It was impossible not to hear my father's voice. "Where are my fine actor and his feckless task mistress?" he roared. "Where, oh, where?"

"He's here," Gillie called, a triumphant grin near splitting her face.

"No!" I said at a scramble, looking for a place we could hide. "Don't tell him what we did, please, Gillie," I begged.

"We'll see."

"Where are my vagrants?" He was nearly upon us.

"Just by the pond, Mr. Junius." And Gillie was off, heading in the opposite direction of the voice she knew all too well.

Conceal me what I am . . .
  Twelfth Night by William Shakespeare

5

I heard Father lumbering through the trumpet vines. "Strumpet vines," he called them. "All pink and giddy with spring." He was chopping the air with be-ringed gloves. Conducting an invisible orchestra, and singing. *"When that I was and a little tiny boy, with hey, ho, the wind and the rain."*

On his head sat a maroon, stovepipe hat, and a silver sword hung from his belt. Just above his boot was his tattered trouser leg. "Hence home!" he roared, "you idle creatures, get you home! Is this a holiday? What, know you not, knaves, speak!"

He was upon us.

Johnny and I clasped hands and jumped into the pond.

"We're not dying, just hiding, so hold your breath," I told him, as we slipped below the surface of the water. Father swept to the pond's edge. Behind him trotted Prospero, an ancient goat with a matted coat and a crystal-studded crown on his shaggy head.

"Find the slackers," Father ordered, giving Prospero a slap on his grimy rump. From just under the water, I saw the goat's sorry nose poking and snuffling.

I popped up gasping. Father ignored me, reached into the pond and plucked my brother out, lifting him high in the air. He was limp and a bit blue.

"My best son, my darling," he said, covering his face with kisses. The boy sputtered and gulped.

He dropped him to the ground and looked blankly at me. "How now, majesty?" I shook the water from my hair. "And who is this?" He stared at me with an empty gaze I called his *forgetting* face.

"A drowned man, a fool, and a mad man," I answered, winking like a sly elf.

"Who?"

"It's me, Asia, your daughter."

"Of course, child, of course, how wretched am I, blinded by the sun to be sure." He turned to the boy. "So what of you then? *Speak.*" He gave Johnny a mighty shake. "Where is your tongue, knave?"

Between gulps of air, the boy recited. "But died thy sister of her, of her, uh—"

"Go on!"

"But died thy sister of her love, sir? I am all the daughters of my father's house and all, uh—"

I jumped to my feet. *"And all the brothers too!"* I said.

"Don't help him, Asia!"

"Go on, Johnny," I whispered, "you know the words." But my brother, the confidante of my frog king, lost his voice.

41

"What in Hades did thy sister die of, boy?"

"I know, Father," I said. "Her heart shrunk up and she died of longing."

"Speak, Johnny, speak!" he commanded. Urine streamed down my brother's legs, mixing with the water of the pond at his feet. "Have I no son but this, who shudders in the weeds?"

I ran to my father and clutched his hand. "Let me be an actor too!"

"Never!"

"I must!"

"Silence," he shouted. "You know better."

"I'll be your bootblack, or your fool."

"Or my whore? Christ! How many times must I tell you?"

"A million!" I shouted.

He shouted louder. "No daughter of mine will ever go on the stage. You shall never be fondled in corners, or wear paint and stink like a harlot. You are meant to bear fine sons. That's the role you shall play."

"Never," I whispered.

"Sit down, daughter."

Father took Johnny's face in his hands. "The verses must burn in you, boy, awake or asleep. Spit them, *bellow* them if you must. Know King Richard or Brutus or the poor lowly grave digger as you know yourself."

"Okay," my brother said, removing a tadpole from his hair.

"Even Prospero there is better able to move me." Father pointed to the goat chewing on the ragged cloth of his trouser. "He's pretending he's a starving pauper, and damn well, I might add."

The goat bit him on the ankle. "How dare you! Play dead, you wretched beast." The goat's legs splayed out. He thudded to the ground. "Brilliant," Father said. He cuffed the boy. "Now say the words!" My brother bolted through the vines. "Oh, sweet God, boy, what have I done now?"

Father knelt to me, gently placing the goat's crown atop my long black, wet hair. "Mama wants us for supper, child. I believe I was to tell you so, earlier." He wiped the tears from my face with the sleeve of his coat. "Prince Hal struts in you, I know it. And Ariel the Sprite shifts shapes in your head."

He adjusted the crown low over my eyes and smeared a bit of moist, black dirt above my mouth. "Now there is a bold broth of a lad, eh?" He strode off, singing, the goat at his heels. *A foolish thing is but a toy, for the rain it raineth every day.*"

I stood on the new legs of the thing he had christened, squared my narrow shoulders and wobbled into a darkening wood.

Be lion mettled and proud . . .
    Macbeth by William Shakespeare

6

"Look alive, Sonny and carry me off. I've just been hanged you know." I was flat on the ground by the stable—in costume of course, my eyes rolled back in my head, a rope tied round my neck. My cap had bells and tassels; my trousers were puffed and puckered, striped with red and yellow.

"Who are we, again?" Johnny Booth asked.

"Lear and his fool, you blunderpuss. And Titania, there, is your glorious steed." I pointed to our aged milk cow; her back dipped low, like a half moon.

"Okay, I guess," he answered.

"Moan, cry to the winds," I shouted, *"for your fool is dead!* Put my poor body on Titania and play the damn scene!"

"Yep," said my brother, hefting me onto the cow and giving her a swat on the rump. When I was out of sight, he scampered into the bushes. The cow groaned under my limp weight. She carried me to the barn, where she promptly buried her head in a pile of alfalfa. Johnny Booth was nowhere to be seen.

"This poor animal, you ran her near to death," Gillian said later, as she ladled water into the mouth of the exhausted cow. Mama sat on a hay bale brushing her black hair. A great waterfall of shining black curls fell nearly to her knees.

"Your mama sat on the rhyming balcony applauding the boy before he even finished a speech," Gillian told me. "Didn't you, Mrs. Maryanne?" Gillian took the brush and smoothed the last locks. "I don't see the sense of that."

"And the Negro children," Mama said, "with their downy puffs of hair looking like newly hatched ebony chicks, watching us?"

"They had to watch, missus. They're Negro children."

"We don't make them work in the fields, Gillie," I said.

"Good of you all." Gillian rolled her eyes. "Lord have mercy."

"Don't be spiteful. I'm a bystander too, Gillie."

"I can't believe I landed here with all you all. Like some harlot of a hurricane topped the levy and spilled me here."

"Yes, Gillian James," Mama soothed. She hugged Gillie. "It was just like that. In a tearing rain you came, black as what, Asia?"

"Ebony rain, Mama, with wind so hard it split the parlor glass. Can you remember, Mama?"

"I can smell that night," Mama said, taking Gillian's hand. "You saved us."

I heard the night; the crash of heavy rain on the roof timbers.

For out of that wind-socked storm came our truest friend. We closed our eyes and remembered while Gillian sang a ditty, sweet and salty like a lick of sugar on a sweaty hand. *"My lover boy is on the wind, all full of hungry haunting. If he be dead than so am I, or else my God is taunting."*

That night long ago, a tall, sodden form appeared out of nowhere at our door, shaking water from itself like a crazed otter.

"A rolling pin, dearie?" said Mama in her whispery cockney drawl, peering at the specter "And a gun?"

"I know how to use both, missus," it answered in a low voice that was neither man nor woman.

"Good," said Mama. "We have slave catchers about and madly rising dough on occasion." Mama smiled at the creature and held out her hand, her rosy face with its pointed chin and her undulate black coils of hair shining in the lamplight.

A woman emerged from under her soaking wrap, tall as a man and black as a crow's wing. "I am Gillian James. A free woman and a wife."

"And bold to boot," said Father.

"I read that you people needed a woman with good strong hands at the ready. And here I am." Gillian James glanced behind her into the storm.

"She can read?" my brother asked.

"Shut up, Johnny," I said, pinching his arm.

"I'm glad of it, lady dove," said Mama.

46

"Heaven sent, she is with the countenance of an African queen," Father added with a sweeping bow. "Come in, my dear, do come in."

"Do you trust us to treat you well?" Mama asked.

Gillian thought long and hard on this. "You all aren't real. Don't take offense, but you got paint all over your face, Mr. Booth, like no white man off the stage I ever did see."

"Hmmph," said Father. "Would that be a compliment?"

"Of course, dear lovey," said Mama, resplendent in Arab pantaloons and scarves of silk. "We're not at all real, look at us." She pointed to Prospero the goat with a peacock-feathered cap atop his head, my brother decked in father's jeweled turban and me in my usual field hand's garb—faded overalls with dirt smudges on my face.

Gillian surveyed the lot of us. "Now that child there," Gillian pointed to me, "that one is passing real."

"I damn well am not!" I sassed her, offended to the quick.

"Are too," yelped Johnny Booth. I give him a kick in the rear and we were at it, scuffling on the floor.

Mama stepped over us and held out a plate of buttered turnips to Gillian. "Were you in the jailhouse, then, dear? As it was rumored, not that it matters a bit to us."

"I got me three nights in the calaboose, missus,

and I didn't do nothing except give Nettie Ripson a good licking for her evil ways."

"Who is Nettie Ripson?" I asked, sitting atop my brother and pinching him again for good measure.

"Bad to her bones and sneaky as a cellar rat." Gillian's face made a fearful scowl.

"Did you beat her?" Johnny Booth inquired.

"Or kill her?" I asked, helping my brother to his feet, giving him a quick kiss on the cheek.

"I gave her a thrashing on a Monday that knocked her into Tuesday," Gillian said.

Father offered a chair to the wondrous creature who seemed to grow before our eyes.

"Me and Nettie Ripson, we both ran the boarding house," Gillian said, handing off her turnips to Prospero the goat. "While she was in the front room cozening up to the guests, especially Mr. Charles B. Jenkins, I was out back with the slops pail. And she had the gall to say about me, 'The colored girl sees me for a liar, Mr. Jenkins. That lazy Gillian, she's not got your room ready. She's not good at tamping the fire or bleaching the sheets white and soft enough for a gentleman's tired bones.'"

Gillian's voice took on a nasal whine. "'I'm a right ready little bird, Mr. Jenkins,' that harlot said."

I pictured Nettie Ripson like she was standing in front of us.

"I'll see her in hell," Gillian said. "We are both

freedwomen and that was my house too. I saw her behind the screen taking down her hair, so it fell just over the top of her chemise early in the morning before the boarders came down for their grits and honey cakes. I was not bred up to carry her slops to the hole in the ground."

Gillian brandished her rolling pin at the wall, at her unseen foe. "You carry the pail, Nettie Ripson. I mean to sit in the parlor with my fine skirt to the tops of my shoes for I am a lady. I should be the one saying a good morning to Mr. Jenkins, or 'How's the gout, Mrs. Dotey?' Or 'Do you like the spanking clean curtains with the smell of a spring morning, Mr. Edwards?' Not you, Nettie Ripson!"

Gillian slammed the rolling pin against the wall as though she was swatting a giant fly. "I basted her good and left the place without so much as a look back."

Father beamed and patted Gillian's arm. "Bravo."

"You're wonderful," said Mama. "Nettie Ripson can go straight to the devil's bed for all I care."

"She scares me," cried my brother, pulling father's turban over his face.

Gillian turned her back to us, toward the storm. "My man is out there somewhere."

"In spirit?" Father asked.

"In flesh," Gillian leaned toward him. "He'd soon cut you as breathe."

"Do you love him, dearie?" Mama took her hand.

"More than my life, missus."

"Keep us posted," says Father. "We know a little about love." He pulled Mama close. "We were fugitives once."

"Stay clear of me if he nears. We're down wind of trouble," Gillian admonished us all.

"Have another turnip," said Mama.

I faced Gillian full on. "I'm not afraid."

"I know." Her fingers brushed my face. "That's what's gonna get you broke in two."

Now, Hercules be thy speed young man!
As You Like It by William Shakespeare

7

We were older from the look of us, by more than a year. A girl courting womanhood, and a taller boy. I was feeding my brother his lines from the rhyming balcony, having been banished there by my father. I was contemplating throwing myself off the ledge to save myself a lot of trouble. Below, a group of very small Negro children, the offspring of our hired man, Jim, watched to see if I'd splatter on the ground at their feet.

"Prepare him well, Asia," Father said. "He will perform soon for a real audience."

My brother was swatting at a mosquito that landed on his nose. *"What is 't, a spirit?"* I recited. I reached out into the air. *"Lord how it looks about. What is 't it spirit?"* I said louder, dangling by my knees over the railing.

"It's a damn bug," he yelled, squashing the mosquito.

"I repeat, *'What is 't it spirit?'"*

"O you wonder! If you be maid or no! If you be maid or no," my brother answered.

Because I was upside down, my father's boots appeared to be atop his head.

"I would rather play Ariel, the Sprite in the

Tempest," I proclaimed, "who is magical, not human and as such never cries. But I am ordered to play this girl who is always at a moony-eyed swoon and flutters her way through the play!"

"It is not about you! Get down here, Miss Pip. He is dull, damn it!" Father shouted at me, the lowly prompter, albeit one with verses like new honey on her tongue.

"Mr. Johnny don't have that poor, half-gagged stand of one who's swallowed half the ocean," Gillian said, balancing a bowl of apples on her head as she watched the rehearsal. "I know he ain't from no shipwreck. Look, he don't put anybody in mind of one dragged from the sea."

She was addressing Father, his face visibly reddening, as for once he was without stage makeup. "What do you say to that, Mr. Junius? Why don't you let Asia show him how it's done?"

"Why don't you hold your tongue?" Father barked at Gillian.

"Soon you'll say how sweetly Johnny Booth makes a lover on Shakespeare's lost island, dear," Mama said, stroking my brother's hair as he glowered at Gillian.

"What have I here?" Father shouted at me. "Is this girl so thin of spirit that he remains but a shadow?"

"I don't know how to teach him, Dad."

"You must, Asia. Somehow you must, don't you

see? We don't have much time." Father looked wan and old.

"What's the rush, Dad?" I asked, though his face told me there was a rush. I knelt on the ledge of the balcony.

"Go on with you," he said.

"What shall I do say what, what shall I do?" I said, making a rude noise with my tongue.

Johnny Booth did the same. We had a spitting contest. I won. The assembled Negro children applauded.

Father threw up his hands. Mama passed him a bowl of something green.

"Christ, the snow peas are pallid as a fairy's wing." Father tossed a withered bean at the barn. "Is there nothing to eat here?"

"I'm sorry, lovey," said Mama. "The Negroes would rather be an audience than farm. Asia and Johnny do their best, but you have asked so much of them."

"Of *me!*" I yelled.

"No matter. The Negroes are godly good folk and will be made wiser by the verses," he said, pointing to the children fidgeting on the bench. "How many are you?"

"Six, then, Captain, with Papa Jim's Lucy birthing a new one this very morning," a child answered, her mouth full of potato. "And I'm the oldest. I'm seven."

"'Tis well, then, a fresh life, a new-born day,

what could be more glorious?" Father said, pulling a coin from his pocket. "Wish your mama many fine sons. They embolden you in old age. *If*," he pointed to my brother, "they versify with spirit and follow well." Father lifted his head. *"Sigh no more, ladies, sigh no more,"* he sang in a ragged voice. *"Men were deceivers ever, One foot in sea, and one on shore, to one thing constant never . . ."*

"Mr. Junius," our man Jim called. "The cows is dry."

"Oh, dear Jimbo, thank you for the fine fellow you are. I'll see to them, of course." Father ambled toward the barn. *"Then sigh not so but let them go."* He stumbled a bit. *"And be you blithe and bonny. Converting all your sounds of woe into hey nonny, nonny."*

Father was crying and I didn't know why. I followed him.

Inside the barn, Father rested his head against the soft flank of old Titania, as the other animals watched him with their great, patient eyes. He presented them with warm barley mash and piles of alfalfa.

"Are you not the stock of kings with your silken coats and proud bearing? Will you not give milk and butter and curd for my poor hungry dears, as I seem not to be able to provide." He blew his nose into a silken hanky.

They nodded and grunted, as if to say, "He means us well, and they will never slaughter us, so we will feed them." Of course, when he left for his liquor and, I suppose, a moment with his fairy, Evelina, we milked the cows and mixed the thin liquid with pone and pronounced the supper mash fit for a royal.

"Lord, how we work this damn farm," Gillian said, spitting at a horsefly and spooning the mash into wooden bowls. "I ain't putting the last of the raisins in, so eat on up, honey. You got to hoe about now. The field is wanting. And where in heaven or below is that boy, Johnny?"

"Studying, I'll guess, for Father."

"Dreaming, I know, for no one," Gillian said.

"I don't mind the work, Gillie. It makes me muscled."

I followed her outside, where she took up a hoe. "Women ain't oxes, baby. And those children Mr. Junius teaches to read, when there is a law against such things; what's the good of that if they catch him?"

"How can you ask that? If they can read, they can fly anywhere," I said.

"I can't see giving hopes where there are none. They surely won't get but a mile from this place without selling their immortal souls to something."

"Your own husband helps the slaves run, Gillie!"

"And when's he gonna get dead for it? When?" She smashed her hoe against a tree.

"Get down here to me, Hulbert James," she

55

cried. "Or don't, damn you! Don't!" She crouched down, sobbing.

"He'll come, Gillie. He loves you."

"He loves the fight, baby. Then me. In that order."

We trudged to the cornfield, if you could call the weary stalks of brown-grazed ears and rutted earth a proper field. As my hair had escaped my hat, I stuffed the errant curls down into my shirt.

Gillian wiped my dirty face with her hand. "You have a beauty, Asia, like a bone polished clean," Gillie said as we hoed the hard, pebbly earth. "And it will find you."

"How will it find me, Gillie?"

"Let it go, baby, let it go to woman form." She freed my hair from under my hat. It tumbled all around me. "A beauty to freeze the days," she said.

"Nuts!" I answered, my hot cheeks and pop-out curls vexing me to a near-scream. "I don't know how to be. I never know how to be."

Just then, Mama's languid soprano rang through the steamy air. *"Says hopping Jane to tinker's boy, away, away, I go, oh, if ye will make me queen again, my maidenhead you'll know, oh."*

"Says tinker's boy to hopping Jane, the die is sure as cast," Gillian sang back in her strong alto. *"I shall but please you for a day, when lust has certain past."*

Mama glided into view bearing a wicker basket. *"Oh, hold my tender body, hopping Jane did say, my maidenhead will soon be gone, right now in this wild hay."* Mama puffed out her chest. "And that was nothing, Gillie woman," she said. "I have more."

"Oh, Lord, aren't you a picture of a wild Sally, missus. My ears go to burning up at such words."

"Fire, then fire!" Mama shouted. "Let's have a two step."

As I downed the pone and milk, letting the cold of the milk soak my shirt, they glided together across the grass, under the clothesline where white petticoats, shirts and chemises fluttered like headless wraiths in the wind.

I watched them until I couldn't hear their voices, until they disappeared behind the barn. I ran my hands over my coveralls, feeling the soft rise of new breasts. I glanced down at the carrots Mama tucked in a napkin. My stomach was rumbling and my head was light. I grabbed my stash from behind the willow tree. "Johnny!" I called up to the branches. "Get down here, lazy boy, it's time."

"For what?" he said. "More damn versifying?" He dropped a slender book on my head. His body followed, too tall for his pants.

"Don't ask, just follow."

I was to say that many times. He did as he was told. And of what happened next, I was ashamed.

Good sister, wrong me not, nor wrong yourself-to make a bondmaid and a slave of me.
    Taming of the Shrew by William Shakespeare

8

We sprawled at the edge of the pond, a basket of blackberries beside us, amid the squirming blood-worms that were our bait. There were blue-red blots on my chemise. I didn't tell my brother I had seen my own blood, my woman's blood the color of cherry skins. When it soaked my drawers, I placed a rag below to catch it. I dreamed I was becoming a creature with high breasts and moist lips—dripping ripe fruit juice over my sun burnt neck and bare arms. The low grass was alive with ants where half-bitten peaches lay scattered about.

"What's this on your chin, Johnny Booth?"

"I'm bearding."

"So it seems."

"Is that what happens?"

"What has Mama told you?"

"Nothing."

"What does Gillie say, Johnny?"

"She doesn't say anything to me, if she can help it."

"Because you treat her like a servant."

"She's a Negro!"

"And free, and our protector if you didn't notice."

"Mama protects us, Asia."

"Bosh!" I said, touching the bit of roughening down on his face again. "I will tell you, Johnny. Boys become men. And girls become nothing."

"I'll get this bristle all over," he said, blushing. "All over. At least I hope so."

"You'll grow cat fur and your legs will be like stilts. Ha!"

I didn't have to tell him I had eruptions on my chest. They were rounding, softly rounding. My skin burned and I was damp when I least expected to be. The heat on the ground warmed me to my new woman's bones.

"So warm, so lovely warm." I took his hand and place it on my chest. "This is what is happening to me." I pulled him close and kissed him full on the mouth. His eyes opened wide. "Oh, God, I'm sorry, Johnny." I turned away.

"Get the worms, Asia, hurry," he said gruffly.

He sliced the bloodworms in two, into neat oozing sections, and thrust a hook clear through them and out the other side. I looked away from the carnage and reached deep into the picnic hamper we brought, down to the melting ice that cooled two purloined bottles of champagne.

"Look here." I brandished the bottle. The water dripped freezing spikes on my knees.

"Where did you get that, Asia?"

I pulled the cork. With a hiss and pop, it exploded into the trees. "Open." I held the foaming bottle over my brother's mouth. He guzzled the sparkling liquid. "Don't, Johnny, don't drop the hook. I can't stomach the fish."

"How do you know? We've never had any before," he said.

Dragonflies exploded in circles over the whorls of water below them. I knew their colors—spangled greens and bold blues.

It was catching time. The fish were high in the water. He put his arms around me, his face against mine, his new bristles tickling my hot cheek. There was a tug on the line as we leaned as one toward the foaming water. A silver perch arched high, twisting as though on a gallows.

Together we grabbed at the writhing fish. I was yelling, "No!" and "Yes!" with joy, or something like it.

"You caught a big one, Asia! A beauty!" The fish heaved in the bottom of the boat. I looked away until I didn't hear it flopping anymore.

We lit our fire, and charred the fish quickly, tearing at it whole—smearing our mouths with the forbidden taste of it. The sweet, briny flesh hovered on my tongue.

"A banquet, my girl. A secret banquet," John Booth mumbled, his mouth full.

"More champagne, sir?"

"Yes. And more again."

"Do I look like an ale wife?" I puffed out my chest. "Hearty, hearty drunken fools, do sneak away and break the rules." I raised the bottle to my mouth. "Shame, shame!" I shouted as the bubbling liquid flooded my skin.

He grabbed for the bottle. "I'll arm wrestle you, ale wife." Of course, he won. We lugged the full blackberry pail and picnic hamper through the weeds.

"Sleepy," he said, staggering. I grabbed him before he fell flat.

"Hold my arm, drunkard, we'll go to the stable."

"Junius Brutus Booth's boy has defied his *pater*," my brother mumbled. "He is drunk and he is not inferior when he drinks champagne." He sat heavily down. "Sleep it off. So good."

"Not here, damn it. Get up."

"So, so good!"

"Shut up!"

I dragged him to the barn.

While he snored in the hay, I asked forgiveness from the fish and for my wanton self.

The door flew open and Father stood before me.

"Did your other brothers dine on flesh in secret, away from the farm and my rules?" he thundered, ignoring Johnny Booth sprawled in the hay.

Gillian was right behind him.

"He found the fish tail and the fire and chewed bones, Asia."

"Murderers!" Father shouted.

"You don't know what them other boys of yours

is eating, Mr. Junius," Gillian said. "Maybe they're lying still and ghostly in their beds from want of meat. Maybe Tiny Joseph, who I hear was often mistook for a child, went off to study medicine 'cause the turnips and darn greens made him reach the window sill and no further!"

I faced Father. " 'To learn why I have not grown a tad since I was eleven.' Mama told me he said that. Remember, Daddy?" My tongue was thick.

"They all fled this place," Gillian said. "Junius Brutus, the Second, looking like a royal with the mind of a hard teacher, grown and gone when them two was babies, Missus Maryanne said."

"Edwin had to hide your liquor so you wouldn't go naked in the streets, Dad." I added. "And ain't I a fine actress now, to the manor born, wild and wonderful," I said, whirling and weaving.

"You shame me, daughter."

"I shame myself, Dad. But I am bea-u-tee-full, ain't I?" I shimmied like an Arab woman in a dance of the veils.

"How dare you!"

"I dare and dare more," I yelled.

My father slapped my face. This he had never done. "God tells me to leave all living creatures alone, and you have sinned against them."

"I'm sorry, Daddy."

"Me too," added Johnny Booth, just beginning to rouse. He was hay-covered and weaving this way and that.

"You've wounded me to the quick," Father said. "I may as well die now."

"They were hungry, Mr. Junius," Gillian said.

"Take care of this boy," Father's voice was soft and weak. "I'm leaving soon to perform in San Francisco."

"Did the bear really cry tears of gold there, Dad?" my brother asked.

"Not a one, dear lovie. I make a pretty story and have nary a nickel to show. Most all went to the first Mrs. Booth. 'Tis left to you to hone the craft and make a fortune."

He drew himself up to his full height, which was just above a cow's shoulder. "See you when corn turns to green. I'm off to 'Sanny-Franny Cisco' to stun them into silence with my Othello."

He kissed us. He smelled of sour wine and honey-flowers. I was afraid for him. I'd follow him in secret, I decided. I was a danger to myself. I would run away.

Take the boy to you: he troubles me, 'Tis past enduring.
The Winter's Tale by William Shakespeare

9

In my tramp's bundle was a ragged ball containing tooth powder, a bristle-brush, a nightshirt, three pots of makeup and my only dress. Father was riding Old Peacock, his sullen nag who nipped anyone who did not give him an apple or a courtly bow. My father couldn't see or hear me, as he was singing: *"Oh a capital ship for an ocean trip is a rollicking window blind. No wind that blew dismayed the crew or troubled the captain's mind."*

The song made me jaunty and less afraid as I trotted through the woods with a seaman's swagger and a piece of lemon sugar stuffed in my cheek.

Soon, Dad, I thought, you and I will be a-sea and then at the great Wallack Theatre. I'll play Desdemona to your raging Moor and you'll be so proud you'll forget I'm the sorry woman-girl you consigned to dough rolling and whelp making.

He trudged along. "For the mate at the wheel was made to feel contempt for the wildest bl-ooo-w, when the gale had cleared it often appeared, it often appeared that he'd been in his bunk below."

He snorted loud, pulling a bottle from his sad-dlebag and drank long and deep.

"That he'd been in his bunk below," I finished the song in a whisper.

"Oh, Evelina, not now!" My father tumbled off Old Peacock and landed limp on the ground. I ran to him. Blood seeped from a broad cut on his cheek. I ripped apart my bag and pressed the torn cloths to his face. He breathed, but was out like a wet candle.

"Oh, Daddy," I whispered, "how I wish I'd seen you on the stage when you were younger and full of fire; as King Richard, with his burning heart, and nary a soul in the audience able to breathe or speak." I laid his head in my lap. "I wish to God I'd seen you as Prospero casting spells and freeing your Ariel; your island; your magic growing before their eyes. Johnny and I have only heard the tales, Dad. When you were bold and beautiful."

He opened his eyes. Hardly was he Prospero, then. His old, tired face regarded me.

"Get up, Dad, we have a boat to catch."

"I have a pain on my forehead here," he said weakly, looking at me to respond. He spoke a line from Othello. One of the simpler verses most familiar to us all and used on many occasions of injury. Perfect, I thought. Now I shall play the Moor's doomed wife.

"Let me but bind it hard, within this hour it will

be well," I said. He pushed my hand away. *"Let it alone,"* I recited, trying to drag him to his feet. *"Come, I'll go in with you. I'm very sorry you are not well."* I was doing a fine job as Desdemona, who would be dead by the end of the play.

He sat up. "What in hell? Where's the boat?"

"We have a way to go, Dad. First we board the ship to Baltimore, then off to San Francisco."

"Right. Forget it. I lost my ticket."

My heart sank to my shoes. "But your engagement, Dad. At the great Wallack Theatre?"

"Letter never came. They forgot me sure and hired that old bounder Barrett. He don't drink, you see. He's reedy as a spoilt flute, but sober."

"You were never to go, were you, Dad?"

"Dead right."

We sat there a goodly while. "Tell Mama I missed the boat," he said.

"Jesus, Dad."

"You're too young to play Desdemona," he said, turning over, his head resting on a moss-covered stump. "And my Macbeth rivaled Keane's. You left out my Macbeth."

"Will you play anywhere, anymore?"

"Some rotter's mining camp in two weeks. 'Take three boats, a skiff, a train and a wagon,' they said. 'Turn right at the Calaveras Saloon.' All the free whiskey I want and five dollars for the show. I play the butt end of a mule. You can't come."

"Okay, Dad," I said, my heart breaking.

"You see now why Johnny must do this. It's up for me."

I grasped his hand.

My father was gone in a fortnight, on a Saturday.

I was in the woods firing a pistol into the ground, with anyone I've ever known marching through my mind. "That's how I'll take the lot of you, tough and dead-on!" I shouted, shooting my pistol at bricks I'd lined up on the wooden fence. "While Johnny Booth lolls about memorizing Mr. Will Shakespeare and growing chest hair," I yelled as another brick exploded, "I pick tomatoes and shove potatoes in a pot!"

As I reloaded, Gillian was before me. Tears were on her face as she handed me a stained, rumpled envelope.

I must inform you of the dreadful yet silent demise of the great and much lamented Mr. Junius Brutus Booth, read the ship captain's letter to Mama. *Alas, he did not utter one last word, though it seemed apparent that he was of a mind to try.*

I fired into the trees.

"I believe at word of his passing," Gillian said, "the earth moved a bit and surely the singing whales was silent. Now what in hadeees are we gonna do?" She looked over my shoulder. "Don't answer just now."

Mama appeared in a sunhat covered with peonies that had fallen over her face. "Wear black starting now, Mama!"

"How could he find me, Asia?" she said. "Think of it. If all were shrouded in ebony, he might not see me waiting on the rhyming balcony."

"Are you saying you'll hear him, Mama, when he comes back? Jesus!"

"And see him and feel him, of course. *Bump, clink,* he will appear more alive than not, or as he was last, the great Othello bowing as bunches of roses landed at his feet. Tell her, Gillie woman."

Gillian held Mama to her breast and stroked her gently, as though she were a slave's baby plucked from the well by a passerby. "He was the kindest man in all the world and loved you straight and true, missus. That string don't break no matter what."

"You see, Asia." Mama's mouth was twisted. "He'll come on the tail of a kite and land right here in front of me."

"No, I don't see!" I threw my pistol into the bushes. "Go to hell!" I climbed the cherry tree, throwing pits at anything that passed.

"I'm afraid, Asia. Come down," my brother cried from below.

"Never!"

"Please. I'm afraid."

"Come up, damn it, Johnny."

We stayed in the tree for two days living on ripe cherries and threatening not to speak until Father came back.

"I think I see him!" My brother crawled out on a fragile limb.

"No, Johnny, don't!" The branch snapped. He hit the ground hard. I shinnied down the tree.

"I swear he was here, Asia," I cradled him in my arms.

In a wink, Gillie grabbed us both up and dragged us off to the kitchen.

"And so our care falls to you and Mama, Gillie?" I said, feeding my brother soup from my spoon.

"That's right. A helpless new widow-woman and a free Negro wife."

"With a fugitive husband, who'd just as soon kill all white men as eat? Right, Gillie, right?"

"That makes three by my count."

"Where is your husband?"

"Out there, somewhere," Gillian said. "Waiting."

"For what?"

"For when I truly need him."

"Isn't it about damn time, Gillie?"

"Almost." She said. "Go wash out your mouth."

Didst thou give all to thy daughters? And art thou come to this?
    King Lear by William Shakespeare

10

"We need a man around here, Hulbert James." I ran through the woods to the pond. "Even if you don't know me, I'm not afraid of you. Don't let those sorry white bastards worry you, Mr. Hulbert James," I shouted into the wind. "I can face down a slave catcher until he turns tail!"

"No, you can't," said Johnny Booth, who was following me everywhere now, lost as a mouse in a storm.

"I'd shoot their eyes out and you know it, itty bitty man." There was a rustling of leaves. "Hide, Johnny!"

We dove under a fallen tree and held our breath. Was it a slave-catcher with a poke-nose shotgun and a noose for the capture? Had his hound tracked him here to sniff us out, thinking us Negro quarry fit for the lash? Or was it the fearsome Hulbert James with a jackknife in his teeth? We nearly ceased breathing as the footfalls stopped.

I saw a shoe, a ballet slipper with a frayed toe that could only belong to one person. And her scent, lilacs and musk, drifted to me.

"I took care of your daddy in Baltimore, you should know," she said.

"Go away, Mama!" I whispered.

"Of course," she said, poking her head under the tree stump. "I put my beloved in a fine, pine box I painted large and lovely with his name. You see how your mama takes care of all matters. His face was pale as ash though his eyes were popped open like a new babe at first light. I told him the farm is bursting with wheat and corn."

"Good lie, Mama," I said.

"Don't dare tell it differently, Asia, or he will know and be much angered at our failure."

I covered my ears. "Stop it!"

"I buried him, as he seemed a bit cold. Perhaps, the earth will warm him for I did forget his night woolens and sleep cap."

"I got none of his true hair, Mrs. Maryanne," Gillian said, coming up behind her. "But here in this orange ball is the clown he fancied. And in this scruff of black sits that rattle-headed king with a cry like a lonely peacock."

"Give them to me!" I yanked the lot from her hands. "Now!"

"Yassum, miss," said Gillian turning away. "Yassum to you, miss. I'se an old field nigger, I is."

I threw my arms around her. "I'm sorry."

"You should be," she said, rearing back and slapping my face.

Later, I wrapped Father's embroidered cloak around the ball of fuzz and the tattered King's ruff. I had to bury something.

"How could you do it? How could you leave Daddy in Baltimore?"

"It's what he wanted, Asia," Mama said. "He needed to lie with his father and such."

"That's crap, and you know it!"

"He's here, Asia. And there, and here." Mama stripped down to her petticoats and chemise there and then, pulling a gown of widow's bombazine, coal black and bordered in rust, over her head. As she sat silent under the cherry tree, my brother watched as I pitched Father's hats and gilded daggers into the well.

"Full fathom five our father lies, of his bones are coral made," Johnny recited, tossing pebbles into the water. *"These are the pearls that were his eyes."*

"Shut up!" I screamed and threw him to the ground. "You're glad he's dead, aren't you, Johnny?" Over and over we rolled, as I pummeled his chest and back. "He can't—" I struck him again—"task you to the verses or make you the greatest Booth of them all!" By now I was heaving sobs with no more fight left in me. We lay side by side.

My brother's eyes were closed tight. "I will be greater than Father, you'll see," he whispered, rubbing at his nose. Blood trickled down his chin.

"With no instructor, no witness? You'll be—" I couldn't find the words—"a damn strutting acrobat, nothing more!" My words were punches, born of a longing. I was bred in the bone to be this boy.

"You," my brother said. "You heard Father in ways I never could. You heard his mind."

"No!" I said, unable to imagine forging a force as wide as Falstaff, as brilliant as new science. I wiped my brother's face with my handkerchief. And there we lay, covered with brambles and dirt, lost and silent. And some time later, he cried.

"Daddy, Daddy, Daddy." His near-man's voice split into highs and lows.

"There now, there now." I held him.

It was night. Gillian pressed a plaster of wintergreen and bay laurel to my swollen arm and scratches, while my brother sat alone in the ice-house. "I hate her."

"Your mama did what he wanted, Asia," Gillian said. "Your papa loved you hard, honey. But ain't no rotting corpse gonna talk the way of love anyhow." Gillian stroked my face, my twisted tangles of hair.

"It is not about love that I need to talk!"

"I got to see to your mama, Asia. She's not eaten anything in four days."

"To hell with all of you!" I hurled Father's masks out the window.

Later Gillian brought me nettle tea and a damp cloth for my forehead.

"I got to keep care of all you all. But now I'm fixing Mrs. Maryanne a pot of soup and picking a willow branch so his spirit can stay close. She is like torn paper. I can't let her die too."

"Johnny doesn't like it, Gillie. Her love of you."

"He wants me to keep my place."

"Is this the way of boys, or is this *his* way? Did Father's death free him up? Damn it, am I meant to ponder these things?"

"It's the only way, honey, to ponder all things."

"Don't tell me I'll understand."

Soon, the lamp was low and wind was at the window. I was helping Mama dress. She was so thin; her bones were hard against my fingers through her chemise. I forgave her in that instant and feared she would die, too, leaving a bundle of tiny feathers at my feet.

"I didn't mean it, Mama, any of it."

She huddled small at my side. "You must grow up now, Asia. I have reached my height of mind and cannot find a single, clear thought in my tiny brain."

I touched her again, her child's face and small, soft limbs. "What must a woman know, Mama?"

"Rarely to admonish, never to complain. *Poof, presto,* there is the trick."

"Does she dream, this woman?"

"She puts a sprig of marjoram under her pillow

74

at night and does not dream of a single thing. Dreams are rubbish piles of dead wishes in her poor, sleeping head."

"Is she as living as she looks then, Mama?"

"Can't say, won't say. Pinch me, pinch yourself."

"Am I to be this woman?"

"Ask the woods gypsy, Asia. But don't dare take your brother."

"And she will tell me what, Mama? That I will die with my fingers stuck in a loom, mumbling at shadows?"

"I pray not, Asia."

"You had love, Mama, thick as smoke. You had love. What will I have?"

"Go away, Asia. I must sleep."

I stood, tall and crying, as she went to her bed. "I'll see the damn gypsy, Mama."

I plunged deep in the woods, passing mossy, shrouded oaks. I didn't look back or see my brother following at a distance.

I was looking for a mantis-shaped being with a face like bruised fruit, all sags and puckers, or so I believed. I was stumbling, short of breath as loam and leaves covered my shoes. I vaulted over a dead tree, its rotted trunk alive with ants. I smelled wood smoke, and in the distance I heard keening.

A hut, hung with rabbit skins, lay half-buried behind round, gray rocks. The keening grew louder and then—a changling's voice, like new molasses, hard and silky all at once.

"Six pennies it will cost you," the voice said. "I don't truck with women. Are you a woman yet?"

"Maybe not," I answered. "Are you the woods gypsy?"

"Annalise to you, girl. Born of masons and madmen. Deemed lowly by all. Who lies dead?"

"My father," I answered.

"You're stuffed with tears. Want a kiss, girl?"

"No! I want my fortune."

"Six pennies." She held out her hand.

I reached into my overalls.

"You have seven, or eight?"

A hand, smooth and long fingered reached under the rabbit skins and into my pocket.

"More!" She demanded, chirring deep in her throat like a barn owl. I pushed her hand away. It felt slick and soft as new butter. "Six! That's all I have."

A voice I knew all too well chimed in.

"I have one," said Johnny Booth.

At this, the woods gypsy emerged. Or rather a mass of blonde hair framing a high-boned face with eyes like ink-stained white circles peered straight at me. Her skin was peach colored and smooth with tiny cross-creases at a wide, red mouth.

"Poor, poor you," she said. "Knitted well but soft as pudding inside."

"What is my fate?" I asked, blocking my brother from her view.

"The boy is splendid, splendid," she said, reaching for him.

I grabbed my brother and heaved him behind me into a pile of leaves. "Stay away from him!"

"Come here, bright sonny. I have a soft bed for the likes of you." I pushed her hard. She fell backward, groaning or moaning, I couldn't tell which, for she was smiling. "Lashed to the devil's tail, the both of you," she said. "Kiss me once, for your fate is clear." I reached for a stick and brandished it. She laughed. "Give me a taste of him." She crooned.

"Run, Johnny!"

"Why?" he asked, struck still by the beautiful, foul creature.

"Damn it, run!"

He stood fast.

"Run, Johnny. Now!"

I grabbed his arm and dragged him into the woods.

"I looked her in the eye, Mama," said Johnny Booth after we raced home. "Only once, but I do swear I did look. She was a beauty."

"What did she say?" Mama asked, her face pale.

"She said we were tied to the devil, or something."

"God Jesus," said Gillian. "Bless him now."

Mama crossed herself and bit down on Father's lucky double-eagle coin she carried in her chemise.

"I'll send her to hell, should she come near, Mama. I swear I will."

Mama held us tightly. "She lied, Asia. Don't tremble so. The beautiful and dangerous lie because they have great spaces in their brains."

"I'll take her words, Mama," I said. "They were meant for only me. Don't cry, Mama."

Later, as we floated in the soft water of the pond, I scrubbed my brother clean, straight through his clothes, until he yelped.

Some days later, I went alone and left apples or molasses under the rabbit skins for Annalise, waiting to look her in the eye and learn my true fate. Or, perhaps, I thought, I might be like her—wanton and somebody's harlot. But she just gazed past me into the sun and my fortune was never told, as though it was but a vapor or a flutter in the leaves and nothing more.

"Can you flee a fate, like a wolf or a slave catcher?" I asked Gillian after waking, gasping from dreams I called night mangles. "Or get free of it?"

"Hard to do that," she said.

"Help me, Gillie."

"I got to think." She rubbed her head.

"Think hard and harder again, Gillie."

"Might be my granddaddy did such a thing but his kind was scarce," she said.

"I need to be scarce, like that—like a man, so the devil doesn't come for us, for the love of God!"

*O heavens, can you hear a good man groan, and
not relent or not compassion him?*
    Titus Andronicus by William Shakespeare

11

I huddled next to Gillie as the night wind outside
the window screeched and smashed branches
against the roof.

"Granddaddy heard a sound like that coming
from behind the door of one of the slave cabins,"
Gillian said. "They was pounding, like they had
hammers for hands. And the *clack, clack* of bones
on drum skin was what he heard. Like this." She
banged on the wall to the rhythms of the angry
wind.

"That sound he knew from his growing up in
Guyana down in Africa. Sounds like that boiled
him up and set him to wanting a fight and he was
not a fighting man. On the night I'm talking about,
a hard hand gripped his and hauled him up a flight
of steps. Behind the door, men were chanting."

I gripped her arm, her tale making a flurry in my
brain.

"Granddaddy," she went on, "was told the password to get in by a picker in the fields. He waited.
After a spell, there came a gravel voice. 'Who's
there?' A voice answered. 'Cotton Eyed Joe' was
the password."

"Cotton Eyed Joe," I repeated, rolling the name on my tongue, imagining a man with clumps of cotton matter for eyeballs.

"The door cracked open," Gillian said, "and Granddaddy was shoved to the center of a circle of men hung with rags. I'm sure the room did stink of spoilt bacon grease and sweat. The leader was a hoodoo man that escaped the auction block by killing five whites with his bare hands. That was Cotton Eyed Joe, a man to be prayed to, likely.

"This man said to Granddaddy, 'Join with us, and you will be a messenger of the lord of freedom.' Granddaddy did fall silent. 'Well then, nigger?' Cotton Eyed Joe said. 'Are you a part of this here saving of our kind?' Granddaddy said, 'I got to think on this.'"

"What was your granddaddy's given name, Gillian?"

"Don't know for sure. I did hear that his tongue made noises, all clicks and such."

"Like some tribesmen sound?" I asked.

"My grandmamma called him *Manumo;* that's all I know."

"Did Manumo go free?"

"Didn't happen that fast way, child," Gillian said. "He jumped off a slave ship when it went aground just off the Carolinas. He figured that to be certain escape 'til he was grabbed off the beach by pitch-black folk who was themselves slave catchers. They sold him to a planter's family."

"Did he join the rebellious ones, this Manumo who was your kin?"

"I believe he pondered those raging men a goodly while, but made his mind up after time. He answered this way. 'I cannot,' Granddaddy said.

"'What he say?' another man asked.

"'He say he's weaker n' stewed dung,' said another, a big, old one.

"'I can't be joining you now,' Granddaddy repeated. 'I have to stay in my life. I got my wife and babies to keep care of. I'll find some other way, I swear it.'

"'Is we gonna fix to kill him then?' a man with deep whip marks down his back and legs asked.

"'Leave him go to his young,' said another, posted at the window as lookout.

"'Burn him first,' Cotton Eyed Joe ordered."

Gillian held me closer, until I could scarcely breathe. "And so," she went on, in a hushed voice, "four of the band grabbed Granddaddy and held him fast while the old man dipped a poker into the fire and put the tip to granddaddy's cheek. After the smoking flesh burnt red then black, a mark like a eagle's claw curved down his face. 'Lord God!' cried Granddaddy, 'what's the good of this?'

"'In case you caught by the white men or ain't ate by hounds, we'll bury you somewhere so your kin knows,' Cotton Eyed Joe answered. 'And you got our mark now, nigger, and that binds you to us no matter what.'

"Granddaddy backed slowly out the door," Gillian said, "rubbing the raised brand on his face. On his way back to his woman and babies he stole three chickens from the master's coop so their stomachs would be full for the next few days."

"Did he find a way to help his kind?" I asked.

"Yes, he surely did."

"How?" I asked, rubbing my own smooth cheek.

"At night, after he was near worn from the heat and work in the cotton fields, he taught the slaves a fighting dance that the overseers mistook for happy prancing. Peach pits strumming on gourds with cat gut strings and a swaying, then a high kick to between a man's eyes if it needs be. From then, his people did themselves a dance so the overseer would not know they were learning to fight.

"'The niggers is dancing,' the overseer said. 'They love that gutbucket music and it makes them work clean. They shake their legs so, and fly up to the air in jumps and stand on their hands and kick to the almighty God Jesus.'

"Granddaddy and the boys would smile pretty and stay staring ahead with their eyes while strumming the gourds as they danced and waited. It was a practice, see, for the fight to come."

"Did they escape?"

"Some did. Some was caught and hanged."

"Manumo?"

"I expect he got free, the drums said so. Can't say for sure."

I imagined him flying over thick pines on his way to freedom like it was a town or a river.

In no time, I too, made a dance. I spun and kicked many a pumpkin square in the middle until they exploded flesh and seeds. What was I waiting for? *You are no true slave,* I told myself as I stumbled in pumpkin mash. *And you are as white as a lace doily, so why do you need to know fighting ways at all?*

I pondered this on another late night crouching beside Gillian on the porch of the cookhouse, when shadows passed long and low through the trees. I watched the zigzag sparks of light that were fireflies and breathed the deep stench of dung, for ours was a scrub farm worked by a few, unlike that of people south of us who chained their darkies to trees and beat them for being uppity or falling ill. Tobacco was master in those places. It demanded hard hands to pluck and dry and grind. Gillian's granddaddy had known the bleeding of hands scraped raw, yet somehow . . .

"How much does it cost to be free, Gillie?"

"One hundred dollars and thirteen cents," she said. "Besides, my daddy didn't want me anyhow. He said his wall-eyed heifer was worth ten of me."

"And Hulbert James?" I asked, knowing she loved her husband more than her life.

"I fixed to get him money before he escaped. One hundred dollars."

That seemed a king's fortune to me. I saw piles of coins reaching to the sky.

"Because you ain't asking and I love you as my own," Gillian said, "I will tell you that I earned it."

"By sewing, and cooking and caring for us as you do for us and for all other kindnesses?" I tried to imagine a service beyond her loving care of us all.

"Reverend Smith down at Mt. Olivet Methodist Church, a white man, paid me for making him happy at night before he went to his sour wife."

Just to make him happy? *To tell stories and sing,* I thought, a girl who knew better but wished it to be otherwise.

"He taught me to read," she said. "I read well." There were tears in her eyes. "That there was a trust to you, child."

"Yes."

"You understand? A trust."

"Yes. Thank you. I love you."

"You keep it in your heart." Then, tall and strong as I was, she stood me up on her feet and we did a four-legged waddle to the root cellar where she passed me a chunk of rock candy like I was a little girl again.

"Now taste the sweet. Just like home on the good days when we cakewalked to town and pastor Frank Mullins was pretty as Jesus, washing sins away like they was mud stains on your body, quick with the word of God."

"What will happen to your man, Hulbert James?"

"He's fixing to scalp the world like Granddaddy couldn't," Gillian said. "That is trouble turned to taint."

"Why is he on the run?"

"He's in league with men like old Cotton Eyed Joe with razors in their boots, the kind that can dive on your back like a chicken hawk. He helps slaves escape clear through the Maryland outback, north to free cities. He will surely hang, if caught. He is always downwind of trouble and I can't save him when he goes missing like a ladybug in a tall oak."

"I won't let Johnny go missing, ever. That will be my life." I buried my head on her shoulder so she couldn't see the fear swimming out of my eyes.

I would not wish any companion in the world but you.
The Tempest by William Shakespeare

12

I saw the hoot owl as he landed heavy on a branch with a mouse socked in his beak. There was a scraping of claws and the high, thin wail of the trapped rodent. I was crawling out my window, down to the yard below. I was taken to running hard at night, building my muscles to make myself fighting strong, in case I was called upon to protect what remained of my family. I took this task to heart.

The tick weed stung my bare feet as I ran through the darkness. Across the meadow, I saw a dense mass of white, stippled fog floating low over the grass.

I heard him before I saw him. He was reciting verse, in fact, loudly.

"Where the bee sucks, there suck I. In a cowslip's bell I lie. There I couch, when owls do cry, on the, on the—oh crap, the ditty has flown from my head!" He was coming closer, bandy-legged and near a hop.

"My God, Daddy, can it be you?"

"Let's have an inventory, Pip," he said in his true voice, reverberating and rolling long like summer thunder. "Your deceased father, Junius Brutus Booth, the renowned tragedian with his glad heart and pugilist's face pouched by endless cups of claret, your magician and goodly king—is smack in front of you. I was reciting Shakespeare with my customary eloquence, eh, eh? Forgot a bit, but what the hell. Not so bad for a stiff."

I managed to nod.

"Don't agree with me!"

"I . . . I won't, then," I said faintly.

"Good. I'll continue." His nose, flat as a johnnycake, twice smashed in brawls and brushed with blue veins, was covered in red greasepaint. He twirled around, a long cape flying behind him.

" 'Tis I, meself, your *pater!* I shall now drink deep from my favorite goat head goblet, carved for me by Lucius, the deposed king of, of, who was he then?"

"The deposed king of Batavia," I answered.

"That's my girl." He took a long swig, smacking his lips. "Sweet Lethe, nectar of the gods. Want a drop?" I shook my head. "Do I offend, daughter mine?" He regarded me, puzzled. "Why so pale and grim?"

"You're dead is all, Dad."

"Shot, was I? Drawn and quartered, poisoned, et by pigs, or nothing so romantic?"

"You died on a boat."

"Damn shame. Death is not all it's cracked up to

be. Should know, eh what? Moldered for a while now." He put his hand straight through a huge tree trunk. "Nuts! I forget my state sometimes. And horses piss on my toes, for pity sake."

I tried to touch the tree as well. I felt it, but didn't know if it felt me. "Maybe I'm gone, too, Dad."

"Nope. You're somewhere in the middle."

"That's just what Gillian said."

"Not surprised. A smart woman, that one, and damn handy with a rolling pin."

Something like a chuckle tickled my throat.

"Rest against this sentry oak, Pip. It will guard you from all manner of evil. Behold," he said pointing to his hand-hewn creation of wood and brick in the distance. "Our nest, the envy of nobles and spry falcon lovers."

"I know, Dad. I live there."

"A grand home for my children."

"You mean your illegitimates? We were your secret family after all, with a fake name that stuck in our craw—"

"Don't interrupt! For there, beneath the bee balm I planted my heart. Though I wept to leave the safety of our Eden, I was excited beyond measure at each new flight—"

"There was no safety, Daddy."

"Shame, then shame, Asia."

"On me?"

"I fear so, Pip."

"What was your part, Daddy?"

"My part? Hamlet on a good night, the damn gravedigger or a horse's ass on—"

"Stop it!"

"Sorry. Now that I've washed ashore here," he sighed, wiping a slash of red paint from his nose to his chin, which was fading to pink, "what do you want, daughter?"

I regarded the apparition. "I want, I want, to be like Johnny, Dad."

"Nymph in thy orisons. He knelt or appears to, *Be all my sins remembered."* He recited rather mechanically, having played Hamlet to miners and cowhands far past his youth. "My fault, too, I suppose. Oh, good Christ."

He teased a tear from his eye and caught it on his fingertip. "Ahah! Water, at last. Things move slowly as dried mud here, damned if they don't. One tear takes a fortnight to fall. By the time the frigger rolls down the face, you forget what black deed or sad violin caused it to stir at all. Why do you want to be him? Did I not serve you common sense with the turnips?"

"It isn't about sense, Daddy, common or otherwise, remember?" I held up my hand, my tattoo— the name, *Booth*—visible just at the base of my wrist.

"My God, the brand. I think I'm a bit queasy, though it's hard to tell here in Swoonville-Upon-Deadland. I don't regurgitate no matter how much I seem to eat." He wove a bit. "Or drink."

I reached for him. "I'll come with you, Daddy."

"Are you certain?"

"I don't know."

"Right, then, keep moving along, wind at your sails and all that. *Tah tah. Bonne chance,* good-toseeya." He turned back toward me, his face twisted and sad.

"Wait!"

"Memories like pesky flies are here," he said, drifting through the grass. "Just because hearts don't break here, Pip," he said softly, "doesn't mean mine won't on account of you and Johnny in time."

"What will happen to us, Dad?"

He looked at me with his forgetting face, which he donned in life to avoid all matters of distress. *"Botched and stinking, am I then, son?"*

Son? I lowered my voice. I'd gladly play my father's son. *"Great and fine and none of the above, sir,"* I said in my best low tone.

"Darkness and devils! Saddle my horses; call my train together! I'll not trouble thee; yet have I left a daughter. Right, boy?"

"Right, sir," I answered.

He spoke as King Lear, a performance he dreaded, as it was surely not one of his best. *He rants and roams the stage and little more,* said a critic who Father later threatened to impale on the end of a spear. Yet here was the mad old king foaming and frothing at me. *Do the dead grow senile?* I wondered, or was it only this addle-pated ghost?

"Come on my boy, how dost my boy?" he asked. *"Art thou cold?"*

I knew the part of Lear's fool by heart. *"Aye,"* I said, shivering, for it was the dead of night.

"Come, your hovel poor fool and knave, I have one part in my heart." He stopped to look me in the eye.

"I have one part in my heart that's sorry yet for thee." I stood there silently.

He stamped his foot. "It's your cue!"

In a faint voice, I sang Lear's fool's song. *"He that has and a little tiny wit—With heigh-ho-the wind and the rain."*

"Lovely, lovely," he said.

"More?"

"Of course. You win me, elf."

"Must make content with his fortunes fit," I sang, *"though the rain it raineth every day."*

"True, boy. Come bring us to this hovel." He beckoned me to follow.

This was an exit line. I didn't want an ending just yet. "Please stay with me."

"I exit stage left now," he roared back. "Good night."

"No!"

With a quick roll of the eye, he glanced past me at an unseen audience. "The one-eyed walk-away, I always did it thusly. That way I counted the ladies and gents quickly, smack in the middle of my performance, to see who was sleeping or dead."

I stood face to face with him, refusing to move or applaud.

"Throw a tomato then, daughter, or bunches of cauliflower if I offend!"

"Please, help me."

At this, the spirit spun, billowed and arranged itself over my head.

"Upon close inspection, you're not him," he said.

"No kidding, Dad."

"Alright then, here's the trick. Speak no lies, tune that lad to a proper turn of heart and guard your mama from all manner of shame and yourself while you are at it."

"I shall, Dad. I am making my body strong."

"And fair, always remain fair. As you are a Booth woman and they are beyond beauty as is your mother, who I watch daily. Her limbs when bathing are as pink as—"

"Is there a way you want me to be, Dad?"

"Straight of limb and fair as a forsythia blossom."

"No more?"

"Guess not. Perhaps you might wish a slice of my great Othello now. Act two, scene four?"

"Go away," I shouted to the rolling mist or the burly father form I imagined it to be.

"*Bother the wind, will you? Slay me again. Bah!*" With that, my father vanished with a hiss.

"The critics were right. He did rant and ramble," I muttered to the white-faced moon halved by a cloud.

Darkness deepened and bats wove ragged circles across the sky. I heard the baying of hounds. They were not near, I told myself. Or perhaps I'd be cornered in the tall grass by the animals. I walked faster now, toward the far borders of our farm, an inky, moonless sky making me blind.

He lifted me in his arms. He was iron. He had me. "Stay still, girl," he ordered. I didn't scream. "Still now, still." He had a gun.

I have a man's mind, but a woman's might.
Julius Caesar by William Shakespeare

13

He dragged me toward a dim light flickering through the trees.

"Who are you?"

"Hush up!" he whispered.

"Please, why?"

"Hush. It's my gun what's gonna keep you silent," he said, pressing a weapon into my back. I heard the hounds, baying like night devils. "Sweet God," he said, pulling me along.

Through a broken slat in a tumbledown shed Father built many years ago, I saw her in a tangle of blankets. There was a rustling of hay and the barrel of a gun poked through the slat straight at us.

"No, Hulbert!" Gillian whispered from inside. "This is a good child."

"Get her inside, woman." The door opened and Gillian's strong hand pulled me inside the barn. He was right behind me. I saw him; a broad, hard-set face made black as pitch by no light but the candle's stump. He turned his body fast—this way and that, as though dodging a ray of light. He had the straight, steady gaze of a sparrow hawk. Half of one ear was missing. He took a bottle of pale, yellow liquid from his coat and poured it outside the shed, along the grass in front of the door.

"The hounds are quiet," Gillian said.

I pushed past him. He pressed the gun to my head.

"Don't move, child," Gillian said, gripping my shoulders. "This I swear, is Hulbert James." She whispered to him in calm, even tones, "Ain't no one else about. She shuns sleep and is quiet as the dead."

"True as God," I answered, my whole body a-shiver.

"And the niggers who live here?" he asked.

"Too far in slumber to hear a thing, sir," I answered. The weapon was still trained at my head.

"Let her be, Hulbert James."

As I must have appeared a pitiful sight, he lowered his gun. "You never did see me. Swear it here and now or I'll kill you where you stand."

I crossed my heart and leaned toward him. "I swear." Hulbert James grabbed my hand and dipped it in the blood of a freshly slaughtered chicken I supposed Gillian caught for him. "To death, child, this vow."

"Yes, sir. To death."

By now I was numb from the cold and pained from holding my body taut as a rope. There was a long silence as he shifted on his feet, peering into my eyes like he could see straight down to my desolate bones. It was not his wife who handed me down a horse blanket. "Set," he said.

For the rest of that long night I sat wrapped in the blanket at the feet of Hulbert James. He smoked a corncob pipe and puffed in silence, the slate-hued smoke winding over his face like webs. We stared a good long while at each other, neither of us blinking. I believed he was sizing me up for a traitor or a witness.

Before dawn, and still in darkness, he opened the door and let me out, his eyes and gun surely trained on my back. I walked stiffly through the field toward the house, turning once to see Hulbert James slip out the door and run off through the tall grass.

I crept down the hall to my room with my hand pressed to my side, for it bore the blood of the trust. I was loath to clean my hands. And true to my word, I never told Mama that Hulbert James came in the night to his woman, though I suspect she knew, as I saw that passion does leave a trace, as sweet as peach juice, as pungent as new lilacs.

"Where were you, Asia?" my brother asked over the glass of buttermilk I fetched him before dawn so he had strength to work the fields.

"I couldn't sleep, Johnny."

"Again?"

"Yes."

"Did you stay with the cows?"

"Yes, with the cows."

"I hear hounds," he said.

I could barely catch my breath for the alarm in me. I got up slowly. "Drink now and start on the tilling, Johnny. Go right now. I'll be there soon."

I made a blind, tearing run past the fields, the baying of dogs much louder than before.

There was a rock-strewn road that led to our neighbor Parker Scoggin's farm and the slave quarters; shacks hung with pig carcasses where half naked slave children played in the muddy water just near a well. I was near a faint and breathless. I could hear the pack of hounds louder now, snuffling and growling. Flaming torchlight played over the ground.

"Get off the God damn horse, Parker! The dogs picked up the scent surely just about here," a voice said, seeming next to me as I crouched and stayed rock-still, afraid to draw a clean breath.

"The nigger's in the well," he said.

"Get the light on it," Parker Scoggins muttered. "If he's down there, he's half dead sure."

The minutes played slowly as they held the torches, the light sweeping above the water. My bladder was full to bursting. I squatted down and emptied my urine, right through my drawers. The slow hiss of it was loud as thunder to me. The hounds converged on the well, their noses to the ground. Suddenly, they stopped dead, whimpering, snuffling at the ground near me, at my water pooled around me.

"They on a scent?" Scoggins asked.

"Likely the leavings of one of their bitches," the other man said. The torchlight played inches from my feet. "Get 'em gone, then! Git, dogs. Haw, now haw!" Scoggins flailed at the pack with a riding crop. At this, the poor creatures spun in circles and ran yelping into the trees.

As soon as they cleared, I climbed into the well and held tight to the lowering rope so as not to fall into the water.

"Dead rabbit or something they must have smelt. I can't see for nothing out here," the other man said, his voice growing fainter.

I hoisted myself over the edge of the well and dropped to the ground. My drawers were soaked. I crawled a few feet to make sure I know the right path. The slave shacks were dead dark as I passed.

I ran toward home, slicing through branches and brambles. As I neared the house, I prayed to see my father. But there was only the blackness. I climbed the tree to the rhyming balcony and tip-toed into the hall.

Thank God, I saw Mama was still deep in sleep. Gillian's room was empty. I went out the back door and there she sat, still as stone in the cookhouse, a pile of apples at her feet. I was shaking and stinking surely.

"Take the apples, Asia," she said. "Core them. Slice them."

I did as I was told.

"Pile up the apple pieces and put them in the bowl. Set the fire to going."

I shoved the wood into the base of the black, iron stove.

"It was a field hand run off from Scoggin's place," she finally said.

"Are you sure?"

"No."

She looked crossways at me, at the black dirt on my hands and face and reached for my hand.

"Can the hounds tell which man they are smelling for, Gillie?"

"Most times."

I imagined the scent of Hulbert James, bitter as almonds tinged with smoke.

"If there ain't urine and such masking it," she said.

"Good." I said. *I've done right,* I thought.

Hours then I spent by her side. Nary a twitch or a turn of her head did I see. And after, never did I disclose my consumption of cups and cups of tea the next two nights and how I emptied my bladder in circles all around the shed where he came to her. I would do it again and again.

Would you pardon me; I do not without danger walk these streets.

Twelfth Night by William Shakespeare

14

A few days later, I saw the light glowing dim in the darkness.

"This is your signal, girl," Hulbert James told me once I was inside. "A hoot owl calling twice—a stop, and again. Let's hear it."

I sounded the cries, short and low, with a rolling in the throat.

"That passes," he said.

I sat very still and watched Gillian stroke her husband's face, pausing just at the corner of his ear.

"I fear that ear that marks you sure, darling man, that ear wiped near clean off."

"What happened to your ear, Mr. James?" I asked.

"On the eve of my fourth birthday," he said, "my master played me for a partridge in the brush and shot off part of my left ear. He did not apologize for the act, but took me to my mama, who set to weeping. That night at dinner after my mama had served the master's food, I crawled between her legs and out to the kitchen where I bled through my bandage onto the pudding."

"You have never talked this long since I've laid my eyes on you," Gillian said to him. "Does it pain you to recall?"

"Not to her." He pointed to me. I nearly burst with pride. "She is lonely as the grave."

He told me his master would tug at what remained of his ear as an amusement, telling his guests that, true marksman he, the slave child's ear retained the shape of a question mark and his brain was left unscathed.

"The shot," Gillian said, "did send a whole life's schooling into his brain. Without any book learning he could juggle numbers and see a weevil horde before they ever chewed the cotton. And he could hear what others could not. 'There's a pile of locusts coming in the sky, fixin' to set down on the corn, suh,' he told his master to take his mind off beating his mama. And sure as dawn, they came.

" 'You going to listen to the other niggers, boy,' the master said. 'You going to tell me if they are fixing to flee.'

" 'What you going to give me for that?' the boy Hulbert James answered.

" 'Your life, nigger,' the master replied.

"The slaves got suspicious," Gillian said, "and believed the master would know if there was even a thought of an escape, or worse, a rising up. That is why his people feared the boy and when grown, that is why he fled as soon as I showed him a box of money at the bottom of Reverend Smith's privy." She did not tell him she had made Reverend Smith happy.

Hulbert nodded. "The Reverend's privy was like unto Gilead, only the balm was a bucket of human dung and coins mixed in tight," Hulbert told me. "And every day I do thank the Lord for Gillie's slops pail duty."

"Did the Reverend miss his money, Mr. Hulbert James?"

"On no account did he know. The man done shit rockets all day long, so galled were his innards. That coin box was buried under his dung piles by the time I took off. He wasn't about to dig to China for no money anyways. He just sold off some slaves and sent the others to picking double time."

"Cock that ear this way, sweet man," Gillian said, "for I know it hears all things. What does it tell you, that odd lobe in the shape of a mistake?"

"I can tell a storm, hear the rain coming in the night hours before it hits the roof, and can hear a heart across the room," he said.

"And so you can ready others for escape before they even know it themselves?" I asked, and thought, *Did your ear miss the happy sounds of your wife and Reverend Smith?*

"All of them niggers is ready," he said. "They just don't know it. I deliver them the power. Them poor folks sent halfway to the block don't have no dung box of plenty, see. But they got to shed their skin fast like a snake so their yoked-up nigger minds can find the path."

"Where is the path, Mr. Hulbert James?"

"Can't have you knowing that."

"I beg you to tell me or take me there."

"If I did, I'd have to slit your throat like a set-down hog."

Gillie touched his mouth. "Shhh, Hulbert James, you'll scare the blood clear out of her body."

He covered me with the horse blanket, and I curled up at their feet, as Gillian's man did not wish to speak anymore. When he was surely asleep I asked Gillian, "Does Mama know he comes to you?"

"Lord no, honey girl. I can't let harm fall to her with your poor papa dead now. If the slave catchers find him, he'll be food for the hounds as sure as God, and she would be marked. And I do so worry for your mama. She is hard past weary and thin as a stick."

"I wish Mama would not look so like a wilted rose, after bearing children out of wedlock with a man who promised her the sun but could not for years give her status as a wife. I dream her whole with a soft pink to her full cheeks and bands of stark black curls tumbling all down her back—the way she looked when she was fresh and new to Father."

"I know, baby," she whispered.

"I will not rot away here in my girl-woman form,

Gillie. I will not have dullness of heart. I will not have nothing," I said loudly.

"Hush up, Asia. Now. My man needs his rest."

We had a goodly quiet between us then.

"I've made a decision, Gillie."

"Good," she said, sensing the thing. "With your heart stitched on his, maybe he'll have a chance."

I went to do just that.

Johnny Booth's room and mine were breathing distance from each other. I listened as he turned over in a restless sleep. Many times I saw his dreams as though they were in my head. A whisper down the narrow hall signaled midnight and still-ness: our time. I crept to my brother's bedside. "Get up."

"I'm sleeping, Asia."

"Get up now." I shook him hard.

"Go away."

"Johnny, listen to me!" I took a deep breath. "I will be you."

"How do you do that?" he murmured, full of sleep.

"I see what you see, breathe what you breathe." He didn't answer. "We'll roam the world together. I'll know what you know. Before you know it, even. I'll be in every play you do. I'll be your boot-black or your queen."

"Nonsense," he said. "Father would forbid such a thing!"

"Are you my father? Jesus, are you?" I climbed

on his bed, my face pressed to his. "Yesterday, I closed my eyes and saw you smoking a cheroot in the tobacco shed. You puffed three times, turned an ugly shade of green and puked in the straw. I saw you."

"My God, Asia. I did just that."

"And I never forget the verses. Look at me! Look to the wall, sir. At my shadow."

I hunched over, and with the high howl of an old beggar man, I groveled for pennies. My shape flickered across the wall, the light from the oil lamp just low enough to capture a gnarled shadow with talon-like hands. "Have ye got a shilling, pretty lad?"

"Not fer the like of you," he answered.

"Damn ye then, mewling little cub!"

I grew tall, and with immense pomp, paraded about the room, stopping in front of the mirror. *"And if my brother had my shape, and I had his . . . and if my legs were two such riding rods—"*

He flung a pillow at my head. No matter, it was my crown. I twirled and waved, the cries of my subjects ringing in my ears. *"I weep for joy to stand upon my kingdom once again,"* I said. *"Dear earth, I do salute thee with my hands."*

He pulled the bedclothes over his head. I yanked his coat, hat and boots from the wardrobe and tucked up my hair. Dressed so, we were of one face and, save for a few differences, one form.

"Look here, sir," I said to him, facing him full-on. I was a bit taller than average. He was not. "I can do this work better than you. Do not waste me."

And in a near-perfect mimic of Father's voice, I said, "Surprise them, tickle their desires and they will applaud you forever." I wrapped his sheet about my body as though it were a toga. "Know Brutus, the slayer of tyrants as you know yourself!"

I leapt on his bed, light as air, the sheet billowing behind me. In an instant, I was Ariel the Sprite, chained to a rock on an enchanted island. *"Remember I have done thee worthy service, told thee no lies."* I knelt. *"What shall I do, say what, what shall I do?"*

"What is it thou canst demand?" he asked.

"My liberty!"

"Well then . . ."

"Well what? Answer!" I turned his face to the mirror.

"I'm the actor here. You know it and I know it. We'll make it work."

That is how it began.

. . . My father had a daughter loved a man, as it might be, perhaps, were I a woman, I should your lordship . . .
    Twelfth Night by William Shakespeare

15

"No niggers or Catholic potato eaters, their leaders proclaim," John Wilkes Booth said, and from the look of him, a man at last.

"Disgusting," I answered.

"Practical," he fired back.

"And if asked what they are about, Johnny?"

"They say, 'We know nothing!' "

"Secret fools, they are."

"Quiet, Asia. Just play your part."

With much starch and strut we emerged from the woods and set off down the road: a beautiful young man in a full dress suit and his scrawny companion in striped britches and a Scotch cap. Our first charade. A gathering was to take place in nearby Bel Air, a "Know Nothing" meeting.

"Are they really mute, Johnny?"

"They won't be tonight."

"But they hate so."

"They're white men of pride, as am I."

"And you fancy this?"

"Maybe," said my man-boy with an odd light in his eye and a public strut I didn't know. "They're right," he added. "We'll be overtaken by the foreigners who come coughing and fighting from the boats in Baltimore or have our throats cut by rampaging darkies."

I pulled my hat low and tried a rough voice, all the while throwing my legs straight out from my hips to make a man's rolling walk. "Who tells you these things, John Wilkes Booth?"

"Lower your voice, Asia. You sound like a braying ass."

"Who?" I rumbled.

"That's better," he said.

"Who, damn it?"

"The frog king told me."

"Oh, God."

"And the newspapers. And the planters down the road."

"The planters? They keep slaves and beat them as though they were oxen. You know damn well that Father, may his soul rest, abhorred such things."

"Of course, the darkies need care," he said, "as science deems them inferior. And I would never hurt them knowingly, but I cannot be their friend or worse, learn from their example. This I know."

And of Gillian and Hulbert, their dignity, their passion burnt blazing red in my memory, I didn't speak a word. "You know . . . nothing, John Booth."

He clapped me on the back.

"This fellow is wise enough to play the fool," he said, laughing.

My first appearance was a success. Amid the choke and steam of their cigars I passed for one of them, welcomed as no stripling female could ever be. I chuffed and bantered as a trifling boy might among the men in the room who vowed slavery forever and swore death to all the "rats of Ireland."

"There is a call to a monkey man named Abe Lincoln, a giant nigger-loving sonofabitch. That is passing evil, my friends," a man they defer to, a Mr. Tyler Wiggins said. "From New York City to the Maryland shores, those black and cross-bearing scum has to be rid out."

"No more immigrants!" They chanted as one fat flock.

"Drive them all into the seas and rivers!" Wiggins shouted.

My brother, rapt, didn't see me stand. "Will you kill them all and sweep them into a hole?" I asked, daring a distant neighbor, Lum Goad, to answer.

His face puffed out and turned a pinkish red. "Who the hell are you?"

"John C. Calhoun, king of the South," I said.

My brother kicked my shin to silence me. Neighbor Goad's face deepened to purple. "Come again, mother-whelp?"

"He's tipsy, Mr. Goad, sir," my brother muttered. "And green," he added, pinching my arm hard.

"What the hell do I care?" Mr. Parker Scoggins said. "My mule shits pink candy compared to them Irish pigs and niggers." He twirled a gold-tipped cane, his planter's whites stained brown at the knees.

"Pigs and mules? Good company," I said

"I'll beat you blue, you little bastard!" Lum Goad bellowed and was at once upon us.

Reverend Clarence Eccles, the good parson who led "a flock of fools," as Father said, pulled Goad back as the men guffawed.

"Ain't you a cocky little fancy boy, whoever you are," said the parson.

"Your pa needs to whip you wise!" This blast came from Mr. Rowan Orkin, who had twenty slaves and many children with their women.

Just as Orkin lunged at me, my brother dragged me out of the hall. "Run, damn it, Asia, run!"

I turned to see Orkin waving his fist, kicking the dirt as he raged, "I'll cut your throat!"

"Jesus, Asia, Jesus," said my brother as we raced away.

"A cocky little fancy boy, eh? I did it, hah!" I crowed.

"This time. Stupid! That was stupid!"

I grabbed a short stick from the grass and jammed it into the corner of my mouth, puffing away as though it were a cheroot. "Them niggers gonna be runnin' our spreads if that hoe sucker is elected. He be for freeing them all, and that is truth."

"You're not funny. They might have killed you!"

"Now I see what draws you there, raging fat men who foment evil doings, eh?"

"Yes, and the ape called Lincoln shall one day lead and that is an outrage!"

"Stop that talk, God stop it! Father would . . ."

"Father is dead. Times have changed."

"And you are a stranger to me. Father did not believe in the yoke of slavery."

"Who rented our man Joe from Lum Goad for four hundred dollars, Asia?"

"Father promised him true freedom."

"Never the lash, children, for the dark ones are human as we," my brother said in a dead-on aping of my father. He patted me on the shoulder. "Here Joe, here is a smile instead of a mule and a map to Washington City."

"Father truly freed him!"

"Yeah, and look who's still with us?"

"His family is here, damn it, Johnny! He's hired on!"

"What the hell is the difference, Asia?"

"You're in the thrall of dunderheads, Johnny!"

"They ask me to recite and I speak—"

"They can barely make a sentence, brother. That's no measure—"

"They applaud—"

"Big deal!"

"And they don't call me clumsy, or—"

"Don't call you what? What, what, Johnny!"

111

"Middling, average . . . Junius Booth's imitation!"

"Work harder, boy!"

"Easy for you to say, Asia."

"I'll speak the words first. You repeat them after me."

"A puppet, a pathetic Cyrano? Never!"

"Fine!" I flung a clump of dirt at him. For good measure, I dropped a bigger clod down his shirt. "Go to them, go. They seem to think you fine. Rouse them, they sure as hell need something, there's not a whole brain among them, Johnny!"

"Maybe," he added softly, "they would rather grumble and orate than fight."

"Would that be you, John Booth? A *harumpher* who grows a belly wide as a whale? Who are you?"

He picked the dirt out of his pockets while I paced in only my chemise top and trousers, having lost my jacket in the escape.

"They hung a negro. He stole chickens," he said.

"He stole nothing, boy. And if he had, Jesus, he was probably half-starved. Those white men are beasts."

"You were right, they're wrong," he lied, still smitten, as he was with many things that made me faint with worry.

I stood over him.

"We, boy, have stages to walk in Father's proud name."

"I have an offer to perform in Richmond," he said wanly.

"What? Why didn't you tell me? This is great news!"

"I'm not ready," he said.

I stood on tiptoe, reaching just over the top of his head. *"I'm* ready, John Booth. Here's the drill. Mornings we harvest the damn crops. Afternoons we work the verses. Got it?"

"Yes, sir."

We walked in silence for a time, until I yanked his collar.

"And I vow this," I said. *"Never to taste the pleasures of the world, never to be infected with delight, nor conversant with ease and idleness till I have set a glory to this . . ."* I gripped his hand. *"To this hand."*

I kept pace with him. Our strides matched.

I locked the parlor door and pulled Father's volumes of Shakespeare from the shelf, their brown-gold, must-covered leathers fitting just so in my hands. *"As You Like It?"* I held the book aloft.

He reached for it, just as I pulled it back. "No, no, no, no, not today, laddie mine." I cradled a *Midsummer Night's Dream*, the fairy Titania winking through the forest, through the pages at hapless Puck. I laid the enchanted tale against the hat rack that was carved in the shape of a nude woman. "Not this either." A volume of Hamlet

113

rested against my breast. "Now, my love, I give you the twisty, misty tale of a prince."

I drew the draperies shut, doused the lamps and lit a single candle. *"I am thy father's spirit,"* I said in a voice that held the rattle of decay. *"Make thy two eyes like stars start from their spheres!"* I advanced on him.

"You frighten me, Asia!"

"Good. I had that ghost's innards for breakfast. Go on! Hamlet. Now, fast before I strike you," I thundered. "Relax your shoulders, flex your arms, breathe deeply."

"O, what a rogue and peasant slave am I!" he recited.

I had to admit he did look like a young prince, straight and strong.

"And? More!" I demanded, not needing to follow the words on the page.

"Is it not, not," he stuttered. *"Is it not . . .* what, damn it?"

I loped and twisted up my shoulder like the pitiful hunchback, Quasimodo.

"What, please!" He was begging me now.

"Look at me!" I loped bandy legged, my tongue lolling to one side.

"Freak, freakish?" He was guessing.

I gnashed my teeth and growled.

"Beastly?"

I lumbered stiffly as Frankenstein's poor creature.

"Monster? Tell me!"

I groaned and stumped about, rolling my eyes, my face in a hideous grimace.

"Monstrous?"

I sank to my knees. "For pity's sake, Johnny, yes! Monstrous, *bravo,* go on!"

"Monstrous that this player here," he recited, *"but in a fiction, in a dream of passion could force his soul so to his own conceit."* He bowed. "There, I've done it," he said. "I'm out of here."

I grabbed him before he reached the door. "The hell you are!"

"Mercy, Asia, please."

"No mercy. We must switch on a dime. One night King Richard, the next Prince Hal!" I demanded speeches, mid-play, mid-scene. "Henry Four scene three, go on!"

"Oh, God, I forget, help me."

"Damn it, no! Our audiences will know the plays as well as we do and razz us hard if we forget. I'll start you. *'So when this loose behavior I throw off—'*" I grasped his shoulders, my eyes boring into his.

"And pay the debt I never promised," he replied. "Is that right?"

"Yes!"

"By how much better that my word I am, by so much shall I falsify men's hopes . . . he grew bright of eye, and like bright metal on sullen ground, my reformation, shall show more goodly, and attract more eyes—"

"Bravo, Bravo!"

He collapsed in a heap. "No more, Asia."

I swatted him about the face and back with Father's comic prop, an inflated pig bladder on a leather string. "More and more." Another swat.

"Pity me."

"Pity you, never!" I pulled him to his feet. "Up you go now, with a bit of Byron."

The wanton lord's verses were our plum puddings, our dessert. In a wink Byron appeared before me in the person of my brother, his black locks tumbling over a high, pale forehead, his mouth full with a hint of a sneer. He pressed my hands to his cheek.

"Fare thee well! And if forever; fare thee well."

With that, the actor Booth bowed with a flourish. *"Fare thee well?"* I held him fast. "This is no farewell!"

"Thus dismissed, torn from every near tie," he continued, *"Seared in my heart, and lone and blighted!"*

"Never dismissed, Johnny! Never torn from you. Do you understand?"

Why, this is an arrant counterfeit rascal, I remember him now; a bawd, a cutpurse.
   King Henry V by William Shakespeare

16

I was not in a theatre. I was in the chicken coop, I was twenty long, lonely years old, an empty egg basket at my feet, reading my brother's play review to a rooster. "He has breathed a fire, surely he will honor the great Booth name."

I reached under a fat hen and pulled out three brown eggs. I aimed carefully as each spattered the timbers of the coop. "He's 'more acrobatic than his fine papa,'" I intone to the rooster. "And fit for the Booth throne."

"Men wept as I played Richard the Third and women swooned," he proclaimed from the doorway, unwilling to dirty his fine suit or new leather boots. "I will now be John Wilkes Booth. What do you think, Asia? Have I proven myself?"

I advanced on him with outstretched arms, reeking of rotted egg yolk and dirty hay. "Young John Booth shows bold promise," I recited. "He is surely the newest star in the family firmament and leaps like a horned reebok as he woos and orates."

"You see, Daddy, I have succeeded," he announced to the rafters. At least three chickens flapped and clucked in protest, as his voice was lower now and carried to the rafters and beyond.

"You have taught him well, daughter, my lady of the hens," I said, in a voice very like Father's. "Bravo," I added. "Go to hell."

"Next time, Asia. Next time, I'll take you, I swear it."

"Sure. Go to hell."

"They're paying a pittance, Asia. How would we live? And who'd look after the farm?"

I have lived a lie of a dream, I thought.

"You know where they show me real love, Asia?"

"Tasmania?"

He slapped my shoulder.

"Richmond! The South offers me succor as well as praise. I'm their native son."

"You were a Maryland bastard, remember? What about Philadelphia, where they herald you 'King of the Players'?"

"The south is a woman, Asia, delicate and vulnerable. She wants protection."

"I can't bear to think of a woman as a country for pity sake—so pressed, so paltry. Magnolias and vapors, lashings and pomposity, is that what draws you?"

"Yes!"

"A plantation wife made of spun sugar, is that what you want, Johnny? Is that what you want for me?"

I followed him into the house. "Stupid little women with the green sickness flopping about on fainting couches? Father's daughter will become a theatre harlot? Is that what you think?"

He did not answer as he was bursting with excitement and the packing of his trunks chocked full of Shakespeare's tales, of ermine capes, crowns and silver-studded boots.

"Take me with you, Johnny."

"You'll be inside me, you'll hear everything."

"I'll hear nothing but the chuffing of pigs and the cries of night birds."

"I'm sorry, Asia."

"I'm lost."

"Next time, maybe next time, Asia."

"I'll die here, then. I'll die here."

The next morning he was off. I was alone in the parlor, eating licorice drops for breakfast, and for good measure spitting them across the room. I was reading the morning paper that told of the attack on Fort Sumter by General Beauregard, a Creole man with a devilish curl to his mustache and a mighty yen to have a war. I should dance with such a man were he not of the enemy and hot to burn us all. *War will pass us by or last a day,* I prayed. And Mr. Lincoln surely would now allow such a fracture, such a trial.

Hulbert James spoke of such a war.

"Two years maybe, and all my brothers and sisters will flow free like the Shenandoah River, if Mr. Abe Lincoln has his way."

"I pray that to be so, Mr. Hulbert James," I said to him. "So you and Gillian can sashay down main street of any town and be proud."

"And not be dead," she added.

I was not with Gillian and Hulbert, then, of course. I was in the parlor with a paper, reading of men who planned our fate and never looked our way.

"Halloo, the spinster," I said to myself. "Halloo, the ghost of Neverbee Castle. Halloo—"

"Howdy to you, Asia." A man who resembled a pug dog was speaking to me from the doorway. "Might we have a stroll?" he asked, wobbling a bit as I rose. "Pa says we're going to cross to Havre de Grace to join a fight tomorrow. So this is goodbye, as I may never see your fair like again."

"That's a pity," I said.

The portly, uneven boy was Lum Goad's son Foster, whose damp hands and lumbering walk gave me the itch. If he knew I was the cheeky lad his father nearly beat senseless . . . the thought was too good and I was near a guffaw.

"Fine, a stroll, is it?" I took his arm and walked to the front of the room and back again. "There's your stroll. Be safe. Good day, Foster."

"That's it?" He appeared near tears.

"'Fraid so."

"Bad luck to me then." He squeezed my arm. "Remember me, Miss Asia."

"See you," I gave a little salute.

"Yep," he said glumly, and backed out the door.

I couldn't imagine this round boy at war. *It will not go that way,* I thought, fool that I was.

A year passed and there was another caller at the door. Michael Sturgiss had a pronounced lisp that made the last part of his name fly through a protruding tongue. "Sturrrgisth." He had limp hands and an empty gaze; any laughter had been stilled in him at birth.

"Is that your uniform?" Meaning his too-short jacket cinched over a round, low belly. His high, yellow trousers with sharp creases down the sides were far down over his boots.

"Fine, ain't it?" He snorted. "I was going to go muster to the Second Maryland, to join up with Mr. Harry Gilmor of the Horse Guard, but they say I have a bad chest cause I coughed up blood right in front of them."

I offered him hot lemonade.

"Is Johnny Booth joining up?" he asked.

"God, no. It would kill Mama."

"I'd take his place in a wink if I could," he said, coughing, near tears and in shame.

"Maybe there is something else you could do, Mr. Sturgiss. Like, uh, protecting your daddy's farm should the Rebels come."

"I am a damn Rebel." He coughed harder. "And Pa's sure afraid he'll lose his best buck niggers."

"Have the lemonade," I said, hoping it would ease him into silence.

For some reason, as we sipped our drinks under the rhyming balcony I couldn't stop twitching. The twitching turned to uncontrollable laughter until I collapsed in tears.

He was gone in an instant after I threw up the lemonade on his shoe.

"Mama, do you miss Father?" I asked as she mopped my brow after finding me lying in the grass. "Do you long for him?"

"As one longs for sun in an endless cloudburst. I've found his violin, the grand old thing. I must have it by me before I sleep. There it was, just beside the privy, lovely as yesterday. Oh and I must pray for John Wilkes. Good night to you."

I looked straight into the fading sun, then, squeezing my eyes tight, I saw my brother bowing and smiling, a bouquet of roses in one hand and a glass of brandy in the other. I saw a full, yellow moon through a dormered window. There was a spill of light over his shiny, black hair. I heard the low throat sounds of a woman as she held his hands to her breast.

"I love you, John. Do you love me?" I saw her clearly, her russet hair and wide, soft mouth with a tip-up nose and a single ruby stud in her ear.

He removed her dress.

"I want you," he said.

"Love me?" she whispered.

"Want you," he said, unlacing her corset. Her

skin was a glistening pink. She had a tiny circle of freckles just below her collarbone.

"I love this," he said, kissing her breast. "And this." He kissed the other. She closed her eyes. "It's good enough," she said.

"Tell her more, Johnny," I whispered. "Tell her you'll remember her softness and you are proud to know her. Or stop there, if you can hear my voice. Stop and leave her so she does not mourn you ever."

They faded from me. The sun burnt my eyelids.

I was stung by visions now and again. Sometimes they didn't come at all. I was he, and not he. What would become of us?

Days were drifting by like so much dandelion fuzz in the wind.

"I'll take a tinker, Mama, or a rag picker," I muttered as I braided my mother's hair. "Or, a Yankee deserter, even. And then I'll leave you here with the weevils, except I love you and never will leave you. Christ, I'm going mad."

"Go shoot the rocks from off the milk shed," Gillian said, lacing Mama's shoes, for she had forgotten often to do these things. "And put your dress on, Asia. Look at you!"

"A dress, to shoot in? Nuts!" I made for my room. Thinking twice as I rifled through my wardrobe to find my pistol under a petticoat, I donned my one gown for no good reason except my trousers were fouled with cow manure.

"Good Queen Elinor says hallyloo," I said, curt-seying to myself. "Ain't you a fancy bit of fluff?" I took aim at the mirror.

"Hello to you, Miss Asia Booth," he said from the doorway. I wheeled around, gun in hand.

"Don't shoot!" he said.

I lowered the weapon. "It's not loaded, yet."

"I'm grateful," he said with a little bow. "And may I say, Miss Booth, you walk in beauty like the night of cloudless rhymes and—"

"Cloudless climes, not rhymes, sir." He reddened and cleared his throat as I imagined Byron sneering at him.

"All right. Well. I stand corrected. Well, your dress is, uh, is, like a summer garden, then. As are you."

I gaped at his boldness and did not wish to flee.

"I am known to your brother and I am wealthy. I'm John Clarke and an actor too, though not a very fine one. This I suppose is a good thing, though I have not yet made a name and may not ever. I laugh easily and am not prone to uncommon rudeness."

"Why are you not in the war, sir?"

"My family paid a substitute to go for me."

"Wealthy and lucky, eh?"

"I'm a Lincoln man to my boots, Miss Booth."

"As am I, sir, to my . . . boots."

He watched me in the glass. I stood tall in spite of the corset that nearly ruptured my ribs.

"As you can see, sir, I've donned a dress with embroidered roses at the hem that feels stiff and strange, as I've rarely worn the thing for fear I'll be caught in a tornado and blown to heaven in a foolish gown." He moved close to me. "Do you expect a swoon? I am not languid and willing, sir."

"No matter to me, Miss Asia. I love your fine spark and the way you ride astride your horse with your hair flying in the wind."

"You have seen me that way?"

"Many times, though you didn't know it."

Was it he who rustled the Oleander, at whom my brother aimed a bow and arrow, telling me he had seen a mad dog moments before?

"You don't mind me then, Mr. Clarke?"

"I would mind nothing about you."

"I mind a great deal about myself."

"No matter to me."

"How would we be, Mr. Clarke?"

"Happy as hummingbirds if you like. But married, someday, of course, as you are a lady."

"I shall not be an oxen yoked to any man's plow."

"My God, how she has spirit," said Clarke in a low, hungry voice. He stepped back, as though in fear of a slap.

"Besides, sir, my brother will think you crave only the Booth name."

"I do. And I crave you," he answered. "I'll build you a theatre, Miss Asia Booth."

"I won't be in the audience. I'll be on stage. Understood?"

He didn't answer but instead produced a bunch of tulips from under his hat. "Are you lonely, Miss Booth?"

Beyond measure, I thought, and trapped. "No. Not a bit lonely, since you ask." I was blushing. A high red flooded my face.

Flourishing the tulips, he danced a little jig, leaping high and graceful as a leprechaun tumbling through a cloud. "Will you be fine for all time, ah, something of, well, mine, for all time, oh, darling Asia Booth?" He was on his knees, a sad-silly smile on his face. He opened his arms. "A waltz perhaps?"

He was a mere stage clown with an unremarkable, upturned nose and a round face with brown freckles that dotted his cheeks and tracked down his chin. He had steady blue eyes that split smiles into fractions. He would never be a Booth. I held out my hand and attempted a giddy smile that nearly froze my face. "I will have a waltz, Mr. John Clarke."

His arms around my waist were strong, his step light. He smelled of ginger and lemons. He was taller than I. He sang. "Lovely maiden, fair and free, will you someday marry me?"

In her hut under the curtain of rabbit skins, did the woods gypsy dance too, or did she howl like a coyote that had lost her young to the hunter's snare?

Wife, mother, child, I know not. My affairs are servanted to others.

Coriolanus by William Shakespeare

17

"Two hundred gold coins and Mr. Shakespeare's bronze bust. That's it. We got to sell turnips by the road here soon, Mrs. Maryanne," Gillian said.

"I'll go on tour again right now." Johnny Booth pulled on his beaver fur overcoat. He was twenty and brimming with dreams.

Mama clutched him. "You'll get sick and die on a boat."

"I'll get married," I said, my heart spinning in my chest.

As one, they stopped dead and looked at me, looked *to* me that is.

"Father left us many damn debts," I said. "And as you well know the last of his earnings went to pay off his settlement to his first wife and the pittance remaining, to us. With my other absent brothers' income most uncertain, our fate I believe, falls to me."

"And to me," said John Wilkes Booth.

"How much did you earn this time, Johnny?" I asked.

"Seventy-five dollars, but then there is the carriage and the hotel and—"

"Your women? How much are they?"

"Why are you nattering at us?" Gillian said. "We need fully fifty dollars to keep us going. You gonna dig to China for the gold, you two?"

"Are you all deaf?" I said. "I'll marry John Clarke and have money and have a litter of little Clarkes."

"Don't be foolish, Asia," my brother said, putting on his hat.

I held his arm. "I'm not finished. It is true that John Clarke's family has money, a good deal of it, and he promises me a fine house in the city of Philadelphia with marble stairs and a great kitchen with larders full to bursting instead of the wrinkled vegetables and moody land we cannot make yield much at all."

"Are you finished now, Asia?" my brother asked, halfway out the door.

"Yes! Finished, done, and why are you crying Johnny?"

He left without another word, flinging open the door, giving my future husband, who was just behind it, a hard knock in the face.

"And of course, Mrs. Booth, you'll live with us," John Clarke announced as he wiped furiously at his bloody nose with a handkerchief.

"Did you hear all that Asia said, Mr. Clarke?" Mama asked, paling at the thought.

"Some, Mrs. Booth," he said, shooting a hard look at me. "I'll take it up with your daughter."

Take it up, I thought, like a hem or a carpet.

"See to that nose, son," said Gillian. "It—" she looked at me—"can wait."

Later, Mama danced through the meadow. "It is time, Asia. Believe the time, as it is time."

"I won't love him as you loved Father."

"Might you, might you not?" she said, her arms fluttering as she danced. "Love can come in wee bounces, not all at once, as it is rare as a white willow. But if you loathe the thought . . ."

"Our farm is ruined. You deserve more, Mama."

"Well, then, well, think of it. We will all live in a fine house with many porches and a stone fireplace to warm the winter. And of course, Father will visit us there and will truly love the large spaces. Gillian will sew you a gown made of live lilacs if you wish."

"That will be fine," I said, wishing Gillian and Hulbert James might whisk me away to the shed where I would melt like wax into the hay.

"Won't you, Gillian, won't you make her a fragrant gown to charm the fairies?"

"Lilacs will droop fast, missus," Gillian said with a patient smile to Mama. "She'll have lace and painted honeysuckles for her wedding gown."

"What will Hulbert James do?" I later asked, while Gillian mixed black herbs for a nerve tea. I trembled nearly all the time now.

"There's no auction blocks in Philadelphia. He

can run those slaves clear up to their freedom, pray to God."

"Won't the slave catchers try to find him there?"

"If the bounty is high enough," she answered. "It don't matter what city."

I thought of the carriage leaving the farm and of Hulbert James watching us, dodging through the high grass, until we vanished from his sight.

"Then we won't go."

"It's a big city, Asia."

"In the crowds, will it be easier for him to hide?"

"Maybe."

"That's enough for you, Gillie?"

"He is my fate."

Her passion for a living man and Mama's remembered heart song was enough. Perhaps I could live on that.

My dear brother, I wrote, as he was in Richmond.

> I am betrothed. Not beribboned, bewigged or becalmed, you understand. Betrothed. It happened last night. John Clarke sat in Father's mahogany throne and spoke of his love for me. 'She is summer and fall, all seasons rolled to all.' He recited. Surely Byron groaned in his grave. Mama asked him to stay for supper of course, noting the repast would be 'umble.'

I served in Gillian's absence, Johnny, stifling a laugh as he winced at the sight of steaming parsnips and spinach and carrot fritters. Mama poured more champagne and the canaries fluttered in a cage above her head, bobbing and flashing their yellow wings. 'Where is Pretty, Master? Is she on the stair?' Mama recited, as John Clarke plucked a honey cake from the tray and watched me closely. 'Oh, do not lose her Master, for she is passing fair,' he answered. I remembered the rest of the verse.

We wrote it for God's sake, Johnny. I should remember. 'For enchanted as she must be, her eyes, her cheeks, her hair, will all go to the maker if Master holds her there.'

Clarke rose and kissed Mama's cheek. 'And may I say your daughter's hand in marriage is grander to me than daybreak, Mrs. Booth?'

And so, Johnny, that is how it went along. It is now just morning.

My love and . . . my love,
Asia

I didn't write the rest to my brother. I couldn't tell him how Clarke's hands, butter shiny, clenched and unclenched, as he looked straight at my bodice.

Then came Mama's invitation to stay the night.

"Get your slumber now, Asia. Morning will see our guest away and we must send him off properly. Father will witness the document high up in heaven, or someplace surely like it, where fairies serve him syllabubs and fresh cream."

From the staircase, I watched the signing of the marriage contract, the wax of the seal dripping on the flowered carpet.

"There, it is done and we shall all be happy. You will be as a true son to me, John Clarke," Mama said.

In bed, I held Father's picture close, making a circle of my body round it in the bed.

"I wish you were here, underfoot and noisy as a thunderstorm," I told him, "drinking your strong cider from the goat head goblet, singing my praises and blessing this union. And do you deem me a goodly tamer of my brother and a proper wife to this mediocre man, Daddy? Am I to dwindle in his keep?"

There were footfalls on the stairs. Our guest, my betrothed, was hunkering in the stairwell.

"My love, my woman, love," he whispered at the door.

I couldn't flee to Gillian as I sensed Hulbert James was about. I was halfway out the window when his hand was around my waist. He was new and not so terrible, this, warm, animal man. I smelled brandy, pomade or was it musk?

Dearest Johnny, I wrote.

I am much elated to hear of your great success in Louisville, and by the time my letter reaches you I will have married John Clarke. Mama, Gillian and the Negroes sent us off from the church in a flower-bedecked carriage. The Goads, Lum especially, ask to be remembered to you. He never did know who your fancy boy was and says that if you see him, please give him a black eye. Oh, Johnny, I did have a good chuckle at that, not the only one of the merry nuptial day, of course.

Parker Scoggins says the war may last years, but he is not afraid, rather he wishes to see the country split like a melon rather than have the Negroes free to rise up and kill us all. Do they speak of such things in Louisville or watch the waters for ships from England itching to fire the first cannons at the North?

Of course, John Clarke and I pray regularly for the President, who seems a level-hearted man to me as well, though thin as a birch tree. My husband will be writing you of his plans to lease a theatre. What do you think of that? Now. I am a wife and it is snowing hard. A column of soldiers has just marched by on the way to Gettysburg.

They are up through Maryland on their way to Gettysburg. They are seeming wraiths, Johnny, and do not appear strong enough to down a hardtack cracker, let alone celebrate the coming rout of Robert E. Lee's men. Gillian and I sew bandages and roll them as pie dough. The sad, wounded among them break my heart. Please come home as soon as you are able. John Clarke will add his regards as he is standing by me, watching as I pen my thoughts to you. I close with a snippet of Byron, your favorite, remember?

I would I were a careless child, still dwelling in my Highland cave, or roaming through the dusky wild, or bounding o'er the dark blue wave.

Your most devoted sister, Asia Booth (My God, I have a new name!) Clarke.

Love, Me, in all my incarnations.

I heard the owl scream and the crickets cry. Did you not speak?
    Macbeth by William Shakespeare

18

The country was blistered by war, now in its third year.

"Damn it, Johnny, Maryland may be of the Confederacy, but it isn't *in* it!"

"Her heart is, surely," he said. "And it's broken!"

"Who in hell is she, Johnny? Your once-maiden sister who is now a new wife? Home again, home again, brother mine. Great. I'm happy as a hummingbird, in case you were wondering."

"How can you live among Yankees?" he said, the very word sticking in his throat. "In Philadelphia, of all the smart-socked, sorry places!"

"I am a Yankee, and proud to be so, Johnny. I'd fight for the Union."

"Jesus, I'd die for her."

"Who in hell is *her?*"

"The South, of course. But I promised Mother I would not." He hesitated, regarding me. "I would not be a common soldier. So—"

"So what, an *uncommon* one?"

"Yes." He was trembling.

"How?"

"They will tell me how. Soon."

"What are you talking about, Johnny?"

"Nothing."

"You have everything I've ever wanted, Johnny." *You, brother mine,* I whispered to myself, *that entertained ambition, expelled remorse and nature . . . I do forgive thee.* "You don't have to fight for anything." I put my arms around him. "Go to your stages, famous man, be guilty but be alive!"

"We're occupied by Federal troops, Asia. Three years of this, God damn it."

"Then go and fight for the cause your President Davis deems holy. Go! Go!" I screamed at him until my throat was sore.

He left me in the meadow as night birds dove at crickets and carried them into the trees. I went to my bedroom, slamming my trunks shut.

"I'm going," I called to the empty hallway. "I am leaving my father's house. I fear I will not see it again." I dragged my baggage to the parlor where Father's portrait, the brimming, glad-eyed soul of him, regarded me.

"The lads and the lassies who dance in the rain shall be blessed as all angels and will not feel pain," I recited to the unblinking face. "Again, Father, what kind of dance should we do?" I spoke to him as if I were still a child nestled in his arms.

"A gavotte to be sure, or a Highland fling," he would have answered. "Let's try it here in the warmth of our little room." He lifted me atop his boots so we danced as one.

I kissed the ribbed oil painting, remembering how well I fit against his broad chest.

It was just this remembered dance, this twirl, his voice that took me out the door and down the stairs to the back of the cookhouse for one last look around. Moving along the back of the house, I tripped and nearly fell flat over what appeared to be a pile of rags, moving this way and that. Under them was a man curled up asleep on one of Mama's old quilts; the one with the thunderbolts streaked across it in bold red, now gone to tatters.

From under the cover, a man's voice, tremulous and frosty, came. "Mow me down won't you, I'm gone as a goose." A hand grabbed the hem of my skirt and held me fast. A matted head emerged. Rheumy, pale eyes fixed on me. "Come into the light where a man can see you. I'm going back to Virginia and make things right. That's what the Colonel would say if he was standing right here. But they'll never catch him. He'll slide by a man, thin like a starving ghost. Colonel Mosby is a hard man to watch when he's ready to pick himself a new scout. We have to sit real still, and look the other way, because if he is to catch your eye he'll start to shake from the top of his head to his hands with fingers that bob like stuck worms."

He pulled himself to his knees, his hands raised in supplication. "Pick me, Colonel. I can smell a Yankee clear down the Warrenton Pike, especially in the spring when the mud is through the top of your boots. I can tear the ears off the bastards and hold the dispatch in my teeth all the way back to the Fairfax Court House."

As the old man rambled, I tried to move away but he grasped my arm.

"I'm no kitten-ass recruit. I'm a raider with the Colonel. He just don't know it yet. He's like a statue of sweet God Jesus, smiling from the top of the woodpile looking us all over. When the whole band turned to the side, their faces away, nobody saw the fat blue belly and his mule hauling a pack on the road. I raised up my carbine and started to shoot. The Colonel's best man saw me. 'Fool, you fool!' he cried. The blue belly was warned by his shout. No one is to shout, if they are a true Mosby man. The mule fell down. The Yank returned the fire. I took a bullet in the neck. Mother of God, that was a fight!"

I knew this man.

"Archer Medford?"

"Yanks fired my spread of course. They didn't leave nothing but the privy standing."

"Jacob?" I asked, remembering his son with a smile like a disease. He pulled himself to his feet, standing as small before me as a child. I had met other men like Archer Medford, odd arrangements of creased flesh dressed in ragged butternut.

"My Jacob rode with Mosby. Yanks caught him, hanged him on the spot, my beautiful boy just near to bearding."

138

"I'm sorry, Archer."

"I know you, don't I sure?"

"Yes, Archer. I am Asia Booth."

"Junius's dear girl? And him dead these many years, God rest him." Our old neighbor-man stood there smelling of urine and rotting leaves. "It don't matter anymore," he said. "Ain't you a fine lady now. But thin like a willow branch, mind you."

"Do you need help?"

"Don't trouble your head over me. I'm done."

At this, Archer Medford dropped back to the ground and pulled Mama's quilt over his head. "Git to Mosby, git to the Colonel," he mumbled.

I was running, past the stable and the sentry oaks, their limbs long, like bayonets. The moon's face was up-tipped, nearly full with something like a rough beard at the bottom. And the great live oak seemed to reach straight for it, larger than life. One straight branch very like a rifle was aimed straight at me.

I had no weapon, no fine carbine for battle. If I did, I'd have been a fine, straight soldier boy, my breasts flattened, my hand welded to a carbine or Colt pistol. I could shoot straight to the center of a double eagle coin with little effort. And certain as morning I could ride fast and hard for hours and hours, sometimes sleeping in the woods with just my horse for warmth. If I donned butternut britches and a heavy woolen jacket and stole to

Virginia to find a regiment, would I be unmasked?

There was a sharp tang of wood smoke. I imagined I was standing before a watch fire. I was dressed as a boy.

"Name?" The man was flat-faced and huge.

"Jonas," I answered.

"Jonas what, boy?"

"Just that, sir."

"Then Jonas with one name like a nigger, are you ready to kill?"

"Yes, sir. I hate the Yanks, I do, sir, for keeping Maryland under their boot."

"God's truth that is," he said. "They got the stink of hell on them, especially that monkey giant."

"Yes, sir. He is for killing us like hogs in autumn time."

"It's all gonna disappear, son, sink into the ground and disappear like smoke on a mountain, and how in Hades can I get my niggers to cure my tobacco if they all sashayed off to freedom?"

"How many Yanks do you want me to shoot, sir?"

"A hundred at least, does that stand right with you, son?"

"Right as can be. And I'd never skedaddle, not if a hundred was pointing their bayonets at me, sir."

"Get signed up fast, boy. We move in the morning. And pray to Jesus your mama don't find out we got you."

"My mama wants for my soldier's pay, sir," I said, inventing a family right on the spot. "But I'm thinking what will Papa say if I don't come straight home? Since the Yankees took his boats and his slaves away, he don't have any help at all. Papa says the Yankees cause him to swell up at night like a blister that cannot pop. He'll be waiting for me to put up the stew and fetch the butter from the larder and stir the corn bread till the bubbles don't show. Papa says the sight of Tulip Hill with no slaves to farm it is like unto dying."

"Shut it for a bit, son, I got a royal-ass headache."

I didn't stop. "All but one African has run off our place and my little baby sister is so hungry she eats apple cores like a raccoon, twirling them in her hands pretending they was maple candy or roast pigeon."

"Jesus, lad," he said, "this is surely a foul, fucking war. I bear witness to the slaughter and take the devil's balls as trophy. Jesus, how many more of you cubs gotta die?"

"I saw Jesus on the inside of a spoon once, sir. He smiled right friendly at me and said hallyloo, Robert E!"

"Shit if you ain't crazy, then." He stepped back, fingering his gun.

"Yes, sir, crazy to kill. I did shoot blue bellies at Bull Run and now I'm back for more."

"It don't matter anymore," he said. "Anything sits better than a nigger with a gun."

"Did I blow out the brains of the Yankee boy

141

with eyes like a new calf at Bull Run, sir, you bet I did. As I watched his head spatter on his haversack, did I turn and flee? No sir, the kill was sweet as I pulled the Yankee's gun from his limp hands, his maw frozen open to the sun. I had witnesses—ladies and gents full-gorged from picnics, peering down from the ridge. The parasols and straw hats crowed as one, cries of 'Egosh, a kill!' and 'Damn hot for a battle, Cora Lee.'

"One of them watching, pitches a chicken bone down from the ridge. It has some bits of meat on it so I grab it mid-air and grind the whole thing to pieces in my teeth. Right then, a cannonball sails over me, the heat like a fire in my eyes and men flying this way and that. If I could see General Beauregard on the right flank of the Yanks, I could tell if they were my Rebs or worse."

"Sit down, son," he said, "and stop flapping your arms. Are you telling me you went crazy up there at Bull Run?"

I didn't hear him, so engrossed I am in my tale. "I'm sore afraid," I cried out there on the field. "And I've killed sure as I'll be killed. Just then, a bunch of soldiers, maybe hundreds or more, gave out with a hell-cry; a quaver starting low in the throat then up, splitting the cords to a high, long yell. I screech back, more like a caterwaul, then the warrior cry as one of them sweeps down on me and plucks me off the dead Yank. 'We're driving them up the ass of their maker,' a Reb said; sweat flying from him in every direction. 'Hold on!' He gives out with a Rebel yell. I do the same. And we thunder off, followed by thousands of our brother fighters, like a wave of hornets black and simmering against the sky. We trample Yanks like ants as the rest flee the scene, crying and pissing clear through the woods to Washington City.

"'And John Mosby is gonna shoot straight through the pupils of their eyes if they come his way,' my Reb shouts as we tear along. 'Fucking well right, brother, right through their ugly eyes.'"

The soldier just stared at me after I finished. Then he pulled a stripe off his coat and stuck a short pin in it. "Here, boy. You're an officer now, and I'll be God damned who knows it."

"I ain't crazy to you then? How do you know I didn't make it all up, or deserted, which I did, just after the rout?" I asked.

"Who gives a crap," he says. "It's you wild-ass boys or niggers with rifles. Anyways, brave is brave."

Bring me my boots. I will unto the King.
  King Richard II by William Shakespeare

19

I saw myself in Union garb, all fussed up and ready for battle. My uniform creases were stiff. I was new and proud as pudding.

"This cruel war's a ragin', my Johnny has to go, won't you let me go with you, no my love, no," a low, mournful voice sang somewhere near, along with the chug and strum of a washboard.

There was a crack of thunder and a dim light in the distance. I crawled under a log as rain pelted me. I saw the Fed commander, all rigged with stripes on his sleeve. *This time,* I decided, *I'm a virgin woman trying to pass for a man.*

"What the hell does a whelp like you want here?" he says, pulling me out by the pants leg.

"To fight for father Abraham, of course," I said.

"How old are you?"

"Old enough to die for the stars and stripes, sir."

"What kind of a voice is that, son, speak up."

"Stars and stripes, sir, is what I said," I answered in a hushed tone, as I lost a man's sound.

The wool jacket I took off the dead Rebel itches. Sweat runs down between my bandaged breasts, clear onto my pants.

"Wet yourself, did you, without a single shot fired?"

"I'm no coward, sir," I said, shaking my head hard. "It was the rain, sir."

My hair escaped my hat then, as it hung to my waist and beyond.

"Oh, dear lord, take me to heaven in a bucket. Look at this, Sergeant. Come to Daddy, sweet thing," he said, reaching for me.

Did I run then far and fast away or stay to unmask my woman's body and be banished to a cook-stove and a life of rolling bandages and pie dough? Or would I lie with the soldiers as a camp harlot, burrs in my hair and bearskins covering me half naked in the rain?

Here is what I did.

"Sing me a song darling, while I hose you good," he said, pumping me again and again.

I sang in jots and sputters on account of the pain. "Sweetmeats in the morning, rot whiskey at noon."

"Yeah, oh yeah," he grunted.

"My body's in the coffin, my soul's on the moon."

He stopped dead. "That tune is passing strange, woman," he said, drawing out of me, "and scares me limp. I got a muster in the morning. Sit up and kiss me there. Again, again!" The leaves were moist and moister still as he emptied with a groan. I tasted him. "Oh, Jesus, yes!" he moaned.

"Oh, Jesus, yes!" I cried, then, nearly fainted

dead away because of the hand resting on my back. It was my husband. I was lost in reverie. I felt faint as my mind steered me back.

"Who on earth are you talking to, Asia?"

"Lie down." I pushed my husband to the ground, my hand on his pants buttons. "I'll kiss you there." The words leapt from my mouth, all modesty abandoned. I was burning hot. I pulled him to me; my mouth was hard on his. I unbuttoned his pants. "Let me taste you," I whispered.

I lowered my head. I found him with my mouth. He groaned. He grabbed my hair, gasping. "No, my God, Asia, how dare you!" He pushed me away.

I shrunk away, ashamed.

"Don't ever do that again!" He slapped me across the face.

"We're married, I hear." The tears rolled down my cheeks.

"Not the point, Jesus." He sat, head in hands.

"I'm sorry if I disgusted you," I said softly.

"All right! Enough. Yes. You disgusted me."

"I'm ashamed."

"You should be."

"It's the war, it unhinges me, how many boys have died. And I have done nothing."

"There is no war in Philadelphia. Mr. Lincoln saw to that. Your precious brother does not bless him at all. He damns him!"

"Bless Mr. Lincoln, yes," I answered, as the last smoke of the watch fires faded. I faced my husband, all traces of the whore and soldier boy I was and smelled and tasted gone to Mama's rubbish piles of wishes in my brain.

"Jesus, Asia."

I straightened my traveling dress.

"It will never happen again."

"Good."

"Never," I said.

"I heard you, Jesus."

"Do you remember our bargain . . . husband?"

His mouth tightened. "Yes." I could barely hear him.

"Do you?"

"I said, yes."

"New York, first, then Philadelphia, where I shall swoon at appropriate times and lie with you as still as a lamb in your splendid house. And you'll manage the Walnut Theatre and on occasion, appear as a well-turned clown and I'll supervise the baking of elderberry pies. We had a deal. I go alone to see my brother on the stage."

"Against my better judgment on all counts, but yes. I'm of my word."

I took his arm; a proper lady again, devoid of passion and straight of back. "The play is sold out I hear, husband."

"His always are."

"Opening night of Julius Caesar, my God, just think of it."

"I'll try not to," he said, his back to me.

But are my brother's powers set forth?
King Lear by William Shakespeare

20

"Pink-in-the-middle beef, for the lady?" the starched-stiff Negro waiter asked.

"Oysters and halibut, if you please." I was dizzy with the splendor of the banquet room. Platters of roast goose and flaming baked Alaska and turbaned waiters scuttling about with carafes of amber wine and French champagne. I confessed to an unaccustomed flush of hunger at the sight of the beef and new potatoes arranged like a necklace on the china plate.

We were lodged at the Astor, a place of carved, burnished staircases. A tumble of bed canopy and trays of scented soaps graced our room. There was a smell of lavender and brandy, and my husband did so admire my gown, a mix of ochre and mauve velvet with little at the low neck but the rise of my breasts and a single locket that held a miniature of my father, with one of my brother hidden underneath.

I was allowed to witness Johnny play Brutus in Julius Caesar. My husband preferred to spend his evening hours counting receipts if he was not performing, and after much pleading on my part gave me over to a theatre usher with a promise that he would watch me at all costs, as women rarely attended plays alone for fear of condemnation, or worse.

It was with a pure joy that I passed out of the hotel, down the marbled entrance stairs to a waiting carriage and into the gabble and fuss of New York City. Though her sentiments were surely mixed and hardly Union-loyal, with a draft riot the year before spawned by dead-eyed immigrant poor that left Negroes hanging from lampposts, the city quickly forgot its murders and fairly erupted with amusements. Crowds upon crowds bubbled as one great mass: soldiers, fancy women, Germans, brawny Irish, Negroes and high-hatted gents with pallid, fur-bedecked ladies clinging to their arms.

I smelled roasting chestnuts. The sweet, damp smoke from the coals curled into my face as I made my way past glistening horses, the dank, sharp odor of their manure mixing with sharp, sweet perfumes. Union soldiers passed me, winking and tipping their kepis at me as though my joy was for them alone. My joy.

The taste of the last oyster I rolled on my tongue lingered slippery sweet—a moment's pleasure before the salty swallow. I passed the theatre, stopping to run my hand across the face of my brother on the huge playbill in the front window.

"The handsomest man in all the world, eh?" The

usher patted my hand. "I must go attend to seating, Mrs. Clarke, you'll be all right?"

"More than that, sir, I will be in ecstasy."

"Well, then," he said, taken aback by my body at a quiver, my heart pulsing at my throat. "Well then," he said, ducking away, "goodnight to you."

"A night at the theatre is more than entertainment," the ticket taker said, handing me my precious paper. "It's a salvation. I do believe the re-election of our President will bring an end to war."

"I pray so," I answered. "Both sides drink to the god of war, do they not?" I nodded and he nodded, then he bowed and I didn't as I passed through the lobby and entered the theatre.

The glorious Winter Garden, a carved and glittering wonder, was packed cheek-to-jowl with fine gentlemen and high-gowned ladies. Of course, I knew every line of Julius Caesar, every nuance and shout and whisper.

"Let them enter, O conspiracy." John Booth as Brutus, resplendent in a gleaming white toga, glanced to the wings. *"Sham'st thou to show thy dangerous brow by night . . ."*

In the amber glow of footlights I watched him, the most famous actor in the country. A broth of boy and angry man set hard like stones in a ring; aglow and blazing. He was so beautiful, so black-eyed and well-muscled, I nearly forgot he was my brother.

"He wished today our enterprise might thrive. I

fear our purpose is discovered," the actor playing Cassio said.

"Our purpose discovered? Therein ye gods, the tyrants shall suffer . . ."

I mouthed the words as my brother spoke them. *"The tyrants shall suffer defeat,"* we both said as one.

"Shhhh! I can almost feel his breath on me." This admonition came from a flibberty gibbet girl at my elbow; her mouth agape as she absently stroked my hand.

A fortress wall descended from the rafters and swung perilously close to my brother's head. He didn't wince, but paced the stage as though possessed.

"What! In a town of war, yet wild, the people's hearts brimful of fear . . . leave me Iago . . ."

I rose from my seat.

"That's Othello, not Julius Caesar, for Christ's sake," a man in the audience said aloud. The actress playing Portia grasped my brother's arm. From my front row seat, I heard her stage whisper, saw the red paint that covered her mouth and stained her teeth.

"Johnny, you're in the wrong play," she was saying, tugging at his arm.

I sat quickly down, my anguish at my brother's unpardonable mistake knotting my stomach. He looked straight out to the audience as though in a trance.

"Jeeesus, John!" The actress hissed and flounced offstage, raising her toga to reveal lacy red pantaloons.

"I think we are too bold upon your rest; Good morrow Brutus, do we trouble you?" a prompter called from offstage as my brother glanced distractedly into the wings.

He turned back to the audience. "I have been up this hour, awake all night. Forgive me."

"It's alright, Booth," a man called.

"Anything," a woman crooned, "I forgive you anything."

So redeemed, he launched into the play, stabbing Caesar with life-like thrusts that set the audience to gasping. In spite of the disjointed performance of the great John Wilkes Booth, at play's end all were on their feet applauding as though their hands might lift them to the feet of my brother as one.

I rushed backstage past actors flinging off costumes, past the clouds of powder and the chink of the spears and shields, nearly colliding with a bleating sheep. The actress playing Portia spat on the floor as I passed.

In my brother's dressing room, barely visible amid flowers, wigs and pots of greasepaint sat my brother's manager, Jared Wakely, his sizeable bulk stuffed into a garish, checkered jacket and tight, yellow britches. He was ripping open a letter, one in a pile of many.

"Dear Mr. Booth," he read aloud, "my darling,

I must be your Ophelia as you are my destiny. I have sent a lock of my lower hair for you to have as you . . ." Jared guffawed loudly. "Oh, you randy little twat. 'My body is yours, take it at your will . . .'" He noticed me hovering in the doorway. "Mrs. Clarke, I am truly, truly embarrassed. Please to pardon me. His mail is so . . . unpredictable."

"Where is he?"

"Bowing for the hundredth time, I'd guess."

The door burst open and my brother swept past me into the room.

"Bravo, laddie," Jared said. "You seduced them again. Wait until Boston . . ."

"No Boston engagement, Jared, I'm through."

"We'll postpone it then," Jared said easily, though his hands began to shake.

"I said I'm through with acting, for good."

"What the hell is the matter with you, John? Boston will pay thousands, it's been booked for weeks."

"Cancel it," my brother ordered, catching sight of me. I saw a horror in his eyes, as well as the fever I came to know, and a turning away. "My God, Asia, why aren't you in Philadelphia?"

"It's a surprise for you. Clarke is here with the accountant and . . ."

"Get out, Asia, get on the train. Get out."

"A Booth never forgets his lines," I said, for want of anything else.

"It doesn't matter anymore, Asia. Leave now. Get out."

"How dare you talk to me that way, Johnny!"

"Right," Jared yelled. "How dare you!"

"It's that God damn monkey king's fault, and now—" John Booth kicked a chair away from the dressing table.

"For Christ's sake, stop that secesh talk. You'll get us all arrested," Jared whispered.

I held fast to my brother's arm. "Johnny, I have to talk to you."

"Not now, Asia."

"When?"

Jared grabbed my brother by the lapels. "Stick to your acting, John, I warn you."

"I'm through with it!"

Before I could pull my brother away, Jared shoved him into the mirror. Vases of flowers and pots of makeup crashed to the floor. "I don't give a shit who wins this war," Jared said. "The Rebs applaud as loud as the Yanks. But you are a star and I broke my ass getting you there, a pretty kid with a famous name."

By now a crowd of women held back by a single guard pressed into the room, surrounding my brother as he struggled with his manager.

"Who in hell are you to decide my future?" Jared shouted. "I get you the highest salary of any actor in the country and you dare to put our lives in danger with this horse shit?"

"Get out, Jared." My brother yanked open the door.

"Fuck you, John!"

My brother hit Jared squarely in the mouth as guards pulled the women away, but not before they'd torn my brother's toga and covered his hands with kisses. As Jared stumbled from the room, my brother ripped off his sandals and threw them at the mirror.

My eyes and his locked in the glass.

"I'll come to you in Philadelphia, Asia. Get out of here now, for God's sake."

I'd never seen this man before. I backed away from him, ran from him.

I learn, you take things ill who are not so, or being, concern you not.
   Anthony and Cleopatra
   by William Shakespeare

21

"FIRE! Oh, Jaysus! Clear past, out of my way!"

A pop-armed strong man with orange hair hollered as he pulled a hose and fire wagon behind him. Jets of smoke poured from buildings above me. Bells were clanging, loud and incessant. I tried to remember where I was to meet my husband as I leapt from the cobblestone to avoid being crushed by a team of horses with no carriage, no rider behind them. Their harness was twisted; the leathers flew up and down.

I grabbed for the dangling reins and was nearly dragged off. Instead I fell in a heap. A tall, well-suited man toting a small valise pulled me to my feet.

"For God's sake, miss, get off the street." He offered his arm. As I was about to take it, he stopped dead in his tracks, staring just past me to a figure of an elegant person I well knew. My brother, his cloak pulled tight around him was walking slowly through the crowd on the opposite side of the street, seemingly unruffled by the stri-dent alarms and acrid puffs of smoke that made a haze where once bright lamps flickered.

I started to call to him but so calm was his step, so deliberate his path as he walked to a waiting hansom and disappeared from my view, my voice was stilled. I turned to my rescuer. He was gone. I walked as though in a trance to the place I prayed my husband would be waiting.

"Jack, boyo, raise the rubber!" another fireman cried, straining to heft the hose into the air. A swarm of policemen and soldiers raced past them, their guns raised. A water bucket flung from a hotel balcony dangled by a rope, raining water down on a crowd of people below, me among them. "Hell is upon us!" an armless soldier screamed as he stumbled past, kicking a filthy leather bag ahead of him.

At the sight of me drenched and drawn, my husband threw his cloak over mine; the bright red of his cravat glistening like fresh blood under the gas lamps. "They are destroying the city," he shouted, pulling me along.

"Who?"

"The Rebels. They make another kind of war on us now, God damn them."

"Where are we going?"

"Take my hand." We ran down Broadway as crowds of people pushed against us. We passed Barnum's Museum, where a band of screeching midgets, hairy ape-men and pink-eyed albinos watched as a half-naked giantess stumbled screaming from the building through billowing smoke, straight through the crowd into a saloon. Through this unholy night, dazed citizenry choked the streets; some kneeling in prayer, some licking at the ash that fell like snow.

"Where the hell are we?" my husband cried. "I can't see."

"There's the hotel." I squinted through the smoke.

"Christ! Is it burning?"

As we stumbled to the entrance, a carriage careened to a stop, the horse's tail ablaze; a hell-struck steed screaming in pain. The driver leapt from the cab, batting at the poor creature with his high hat.

"Water, for pity sake. Save my animal!" He grabbed at a wooden bucket that was being hoisted to the balcony of the hotel. The bucket tipped, spilling the water onto the street. By now the horse was rolling on the cobblestone, flames licking at his back. I pulled off my cloak and threw it over the poor horse. It took fire immediately. I dropped to my knees, pounding at the flaming mass.

"Asia, leave it!" My husband yanked me to my feet. "This way!"

The door of the hotel was flung open and I was pushed inside. I pressed against the thick, etched glass window as the fire had its way with the horse. The carriage man sat, head in hands on the curb.

I smelled violets, incongruent against the acrid smoke around us. The crowd milled about the lobby, listening as one for an order, a rescue. A perfectly clean, white-gloved hand took my soot-covered one.

"Go now, Miss Asia," a soft, genderless voice said in an accent that was surely southern. When I turned to face the being, he or she was gone.

We waited. "The blaze above is doused," a man announced. "It's safe to go up the staircase. All to follow me."

We were ushered to our room past masses of travel trunks piled in the hall. Children tore this way and that, the excitement reddening their cheeks, bundled tight, some with top hats and bonnets doubled over their heads.

We packed quickly, all the while peering from the hotel window to the streets below, near empty of people. I stared at the charred ruin of the horse, now a blackened mass of hair, flesh and leather.

I didn't think of walls of fire and a devil that licked at the city with a hot red tongue. One image above all others was embedded in my brain, that of my brother calmly walking tall like a general from a field of blood without so much as a look back.

Crowds of people jammed the train cars, a-jangle with rumors of the Rebels who came in the night to kill them. Detectives from Mr. Pinkerton's force and armed soldiers roamed the depot, peering at every man who passed. A government decree ordering every southern man to declare himself as such was bellowed from bullhorns. There was a mighty exodus of high stepping gentry who believed their world was sure to end.

"How in the name of heaven did them *debbils* get into the city?" asked the porter as he took our bags.

"I'm told they came over the suspension bridge from Canada like rats bearing the plague," my husband answered. The train belched smoke in our faces as we struggled to grasp the boarding rail.

"It's punishment then?" a passenger said.

"For what? We've done nothing," my husband answered.

"For the whole stinking war and the ruin of their land." Another chimed in. "Maybe it's the loss of their niggers what fired them so."

"Oh, EEE-mancipation, damned in all its forms!" At this bellow, a porcine gent spat tobacco on the floor of the train car.

"And so they seek to burn down the city?" whined a woman clutching a baby and reeking of alcohol. "What manner of demons are they, still loose among us?" She whimpered, staggering to her seat.

I peered through the smoked glass of the train window. Was my brother walking near in a greatcoat or armored as a knight to fight a strange new war? Dear God, I couldn't think of such things. Father's lullaby would have to do. I heard it clearly above the gabble of the wheels on the track. *Shoe and pepper fires eat the moon each night. Make a wish upon the smoke, it is a holy sight.*

The morning papers we reached for through the

windows at Baltimore confirmed that a band of Confederates were dispatched from Canada to burn New York to the ground by setting nineteen hotels and the Barnum Museum ablaze. They used Greek fire, the papers said; a deadly liquid that needed air to burn and once ignited, was unstoppable.

"But in haste, the devils closed tight the doors and windows of the rooms, thereby depriving the fires of oxygen. By this providence, the city's utter destruction was spared," my husband read aloud.

In haste my brother left this city. Why on earth did he not take me with him?

We arrived at my Philadelphia home, a place of elaborate ironwork and fine brick, looming stately yet forbidding over a tree-lined alleyway. It was not a mansion at all. Rather it was a large townhouse with four floors and narrow, winding hallways that seemed to lead nowhere. *I am lost in this place,* I mused.

"Would you rather have been left in the ash, daughter," I imagined my father saying, "of my shoe and pepper fire?"

Perhaps, Father, I thought, while I waited for Gillian and Mama to arrive on the afternoon train; waited for my dotty, dreaming mama and the other woman I loved best in the world.

"Please come to her, Hulbert James," I said. "Or secret Rebels all," I whispered, "burn this city too."

What's your name, sir? Of what condition are you, and of what place?
Henry IV, Part 2 by William Shakespeare

22

"Up now, Manumo." Gillian slipped a wad of paper into the leather pouch on the pigeon's foot. The bird's chest feathers ruffled. He eyed the sky.

We had been there a week and I'd come upon her, kneeling before a small coop hidden under the tall chimneys that thrust through our roof.

"This is how you communicate with Hulbert James, Gillie?"

"Just how," she said, pulling a silken-feathered bird from the coop.

"Is Hulbert near?"

"I'll know that sure when he is. Just keep your man away."

"He's too busy with his business, Gillie."

"Some of Hulbert's people have escaped through to Canada."

"On the underground?"

"Last bunch came through here, was not caught, not a one. My man did put them through to freedom."

"I'll pray for him."

She took my hand. "Pray for yourself," she said. "Straight now, at it!" She released the bird.

At her command, it soared high above the city, a fleet-winged blot of gray against the sun. I watched it until I was nearly blind with dots and sparkles in my eyes. The smokestacks of Philadelphia were as skinless as white tufted herons, spattered with grime, craning their hot necks over the city.

I was not at one with this place, teeming, as it was filled with pious women who looked down on those of distant lineage. They appeared horrified that Gillian and I walked arm in arm as equals, and shunned me openly.

Of the husbands of those women, I knew little except that they evinced a longing to be arrayed in the powdered wigs of the founders, fancying themselves great orators birthing a nation in spite of their vapid conversation and puffed bellies that barely fit in our chairs.

John Clarke did well in this place. His theatre flourished and we wanted for little. "Our children will prosper here and be schooled in the ways of true gentlemen," he told me.

Will they oil their hair and bore us blue with their prattle? I mused. *Will they become angry men with balloon breasted wives?*

"Of course they will, husband," I said.

He would serve up our fiery escape from New York with the roast goose to our enthralled guests this evening, he told me.

As I was dismounting from a long horseback

ride, one where I'd begged Gillian to let me go a short ways with her just till she met Hulbert's man who'd see her to him, my brother appeared, his face unshaven, his eyes ringed with shadows.

"Jesus, Asia, I couldn't find you at first. Jesus!"

I didn't press him as to where he'd been. I didn't want to know. I didn't succeed. "You knew of the fires, Johnny."

"Yes."

He turned on his heel and began to mount his horse.

"Stay, Johnny."

"You are safe," he said, looking through me. "That's all that matters."

"Stay."

He never meant to leave. I decided this as he was back at my side without hesitation. He took a deep breath as if sizing me. "I need a promise from you, Asia."

"What?"

"I'm going back to Canada."

"To perform?" I asked wanly.

"In part."

"What part?"

"Asia, stop. This is not a parlor game." He gripped my hands. "I need you."

"And I need you, Johnny."

"Let me stay the night, Asia."

"We have dinner guests. Will you offend Clarke with your Rebel talk?"

He traced the tattoo on his hand, and then held mine against his own. "You want to be a player?"

"My God, you know I do."

"Then we will perform together," he said.

"So this is my sweet liberty? John Wilkes and Asia Booth on the stage, proclaiming the bard's verses as they were meant to be, this is to be my new life?"

"Tonight," he answered, his cheek against mine.

My heart sank. "For the dinner guests? For the corpulent Philadelphia prigs who gorge at our table? Bah!"

"No, no that."

As Ariel the sprite, maker of magic yet still a slave, I asked, *What shall I do, say what, what shall I do?"*

"Go with me now to my tent, where you shall see how hardly I was drawn into this war . . ." he replied.

"Is there more toil? Since thou dost give me pains, let me remember thee what thou has promised! Do what you promised!" I shouted.

My brother put his hand to my lips. *"Go with me and see what I can show in this."*

"I will. You know I will."

"The greenhouse, then, Asia?"

"Yes, yes, later, after dinner, after . . ."

"Asia!" My husband called through his bullhorn, a measure he had adopted as I was often far from his voice. "Our guests are arriving, where are you?"

I grasped Johnny's hand. "Tell me of my role. Tell me I am of import and I will do what I was meant to do." I stared into his eyes. "I see myself. My God, Johnny, I see myself new."

"Asia! Come now. They're here," my husband shouted.

Light as air I was. "I'm ready, boy, ready for these stranger guests who are to sit at table and complain of agues and moneylenders—"

"While a war rages terrible," Johnny said, "and yet never grazes their fine coats and gowns. I'm in a foreign land."

"That must be Dr. Miller and his tub of a consort approaching," I said as I watched a poplar-tall, elegant man alight from his coach followed by a dumpling in woman's dress. "Ooooh, gawd. He's new to me, and she appears to have great capacity. Extra goose on the plate, I'll warrant." I puffed out my cheeks and squatted low, my voice a simper. "My word, dear Mr. Booth, how you enchant me."

I waddled toward the house, happy beyond measure and full of hope.

In the dining room, our guests were riveted, as my husband embroidered our escape from New York City.

"The flames leapt as high as lamp posts, and we nearly perished," he told our hushed assemblage

"Men came in the night, quick as hounds of hell. Of course, I couldn't see my wife through the

166

ashes. I pushed through burning timbers to reach her, past squalling freaks at Barnum's while looters smashed the glass of every store on Fifth Avenue."

My brother said quietly, "Hotels simmered, that's all. There was no great fire, no smashing of anything. They failed."

My husband raised his glass. "To failure then, in all her permutations."

"Here, here!" The toast went round. "To the end of the war!"

"To Mr. Lincoln, bless him!" my husband shouted.

My brother bowed his head.

"How in hell did you get out of the city, Booth?" my husband asked.

"What did you say?" My brother looked wearily at him.

"How did you make your escape, Booth?"

"My escape?"

"Yes, for Christ's sake, how?"

"To my good fortune," my brother said slowly, "a fellow actor's carriage was there at just the right moment. I could hardly refuse, even though I feared for you," he said, looking straight at me.

"I protected my wife," said Clarke.

"Stinking Rebels," the woman to my right murmured. I was unable to remember her first name, as she had a face that faded as quickly as a doused flame, her nose and mouth meeting like a gray-beaked wren.

"And so Rebels are only such if they are not in agreement with this reign?" John Booth asked.

"Sir, a king is never what we voted," my husband said. He kept at my brother. "Who is a king, sir?"

"You know damn well who!" my brother snapped.

"No human hand can save a nation," the doctor said. "We learned that when our President prevented secession of our dear Maryland."

"For all the right reasons, Dr. Miller," my husband replied. "Otherwise the Rebels would have raised their flag over Washington City."

"Only God," his wife murmured.

"Only God of course," I added. "Husband, please, keep on with your story of our escape, when you were so very brave."

At that, my husband stood. "We raced to the trains through the panicked hoards! The smoke was thick in the streets and we were in grave danger."

Were there goose bumps on the fat bejeweled arms of Mrs. Miller, who pressed her warm pink flesh against mine? "Gracious, what a calamity," she nattered. "I'd have perished of fright surely."

"Good thing the theatre was spared, eh, Booth?" my husband said. "Of course it is fact that New York is in the keep of fire-eaters and Rebels. Their damn governor probably abetted the whole affair."

"I no longer have a country," my brother said in a soft, sad voice.

"The United States is your country, young man," my husband growled.

"Damn the United States, then, sir, damn her to Hell."

My husband threw his glass on the floor and raised his fist. "Shut your traitor mouth!"

"Johnny, please," I begged.

"You son of a bitch!" my husband shouted.

"Stop it, both of you!" I stepped between them.

"Act another part, you coward!" My husband pushed me away and closed in on my brother. All at the table rose.

"Stand down, Booth!" Dr. Miller ordered. "And you too, John Clarke. For Christ's sake, we are civilized, are we not?"

There was a mighty silence, the clink of forks on the plates, the chime of the great mantel clock.

"You would desert your loyal audiences, Wilkes?" Stoddard Ridgeway asked; a man who fawned as well as he falsified my husband's accounts. The goose carcass glowed a fierce white in the candle flame.

"What of your breathless hordes that clamor for you each night?" the doctor asked.

John Booth's eyes met mine. *Soon I will be free.* My hand shook as I returned to my seat. "They don't matter anymore," Johnny said. "The South's wretched plight is all that matters."

"To who, for Christ's sake?" demanded my husband.

"To me, sir, to me, to Maryland. Sold by a single vote to the Union, sold like a pile of snuff!" I kicked my brother's leg under the table. He didn't react. Perhaps the brandy numbed his limb. "My God," he whispered, "how she has suffered."

Did he mean me, who lied and moaned in the keep of a man I did not love?

"The South is raped and left for dead," John Booth said.

"Booth, I pray you stop." This plea came from Dr. Miller, who I supposed, would attend me in the birth of my child. I hoped he had the knowing hands of a midwife, as he showed the calm repose of a shepherd. "Your sentiments and your pride is notable, Booth. To be sure you are a patriot . . . of a certain cloth."

My brother regarded him evenly and sat.

"Your obsession with the South is intolerable!" my husband said, baiting still.

"The South fed me, sir."

"Spare me, they applaud hog-calling as well."

"And what of the prisoners of war, dying by the thousands from malaria for want of a single dose of quinine?" My brother pushed back his chair. "Your Lincoln doesn't give a damn about their suffering!"

Dr. Miller held my brother's arm. "Calm yourself, sir. Now."

My husband rose, his eyes were hard and hate-filled. "Damn you! Lincoln is a good man."

"A good man?" my brother countered. "He ordered Sherman to leave no tree between Memphis and the sea. Stinking war criminal!"

I reached toward my brother. "Johnny, stop!"

"Go to hell, Booth!" my husband raged.

Dr. Miller grabbed my brother's arm again. "I insist you to stop, sir." His voice was not raised yet it stilled my brother again. I thanked God for this reasonable man.

"Johnny, might you recite some Byron?" I asked shrilly.

My brother heaved a sigh. "It is too late for verse, Asia."

My husband glared at him. "If you are so hide-bound to the struggle, why the hell didn't you fight, brother-in-law?"

"You know he promised Mama he would not," I said, turning to Mrs. Miller, who looked near to screaming. "More brandy, Mrs. Miller?"

"God, yes." She poured the liquor over her glass and onto the table.

My husband would not stop. "He's a coward who will play Father Christmas to my sons and howl at the moon!"

"Please, husband. No more."

"And you encourage him, Asia. You always have!"

"Leave her alone," my brother said.

My husband threw open the dining room door. "Get out of my house!"

171

"This is the home of my sister and her child. I will come as long as she will have me, sir."

"Such a firebrand, that brother of yours," said the doctor's wife. "He talks secesh, but I don't believe him." She laughed lightly, likely remembering the silk of my brother's moustache, his lips, as they brushed her hand.

"I am going to my room," my brother said, turning his back on my husband and walking from the table. "Please excuse me."

"Son of a bitch!" my husband shouted.

"Let it be, Clarke," Dr. Miller said. "Tell us more of your remarkable escape from New York."

"I'd sooner be on the battlefield, Doctor. At least there, the enemy is visible."

I rose, unable to swallow the fear rising in my throat. *Soon,* I thought, *soon.* "I'll see about our dessert."

Over baked Alaska and endless cigars, the dinner dragged on. By now our guests were spent, with the exception of Dr. Miller, who fixed his gaze on the spot where my brother passed on the stairs.

"Such passion, eh, Clarke?" Ridgeway said.

"I feel ill," announced Dr. Miller's wife, wiping a puddle of sweat from her neck.

I watched the mantel clock, willing it to be eleven. My husband's guests well knew our revels, as he called them, ended promptly at that hour. I climbed the stairs, pausing long enough to see my brother singing softly to himself.

"But when I came to man's estate, with hey ho, the wind and the rain," he sang as he looked up at me. *" 'Gainst knaves and thieves men shut their gate, for the rain it raineth every day.* Goodnight, my dear sister," he said loudly, as I lingered in the doorway.

In our bedroom, my husband was slumped in a chair, his head in his hands. "He is banned from this house. Do you understand?"

I didn't answer or plead but undressed in front of him instead of behind the dressing screen, as was my habit. I slowly removed my dress and loosened my stays one by one, my eyes never leaving his face. My silk chemise slipped easily over my head. Naked, I removed the pins from my hair and held the hairbrush out to him.

"Would you?"

"Would I what?"

"My hair, please."

My husband took the brush, gingerly passing it thorough my hair. There was a long silence as he brushed and brushed.

"Beautiful," he said at a whisper. "But she is not mine, you see."

I bowed my head.

"I thought you could love me, Asia. God, how I wished it so." His eyes were with tears. I touched his face. I kissed his mouth.

"I'll try."

"Try?"

"Yes."

"My God, will you?"

"I promise."

My husband touched my breast. Tears rolled down his cheeks. I'd never seen him cry. "I love you, Asia."

I went to the bed and held out my arms.

Let 'em enter. They are the faction. O conspiracy,
Sham'st thou to show thy dang'rous brow by night.
Julius Caesar by William Shakespeare

23

The heavy snores of my husband were a liberation. I put on my dressing gown and slipped from the room. In the close, damp air of the greenhouse, orchid blooms burst purple and black-tinged yellow. I breathed deeply of the loam and black earth. It was here I planted coneflower and lilac bulbs from our farm. It was here that I came to remember all our summers. I faced Johnny nervous as a new bride.

John Booth was arranging his traveling bag. My little tortoise-shell cat purred and wound herself around his leg. He stroked her, speaking just loud enough for me to hear. "There, love, if I don't see you again, your hair at this moment looks like ermine as it drapes just so."

He wrapped a derringer in a sock, its snub nose just covered yet within reach. He took out several papers. "I want you to have these oil company deeds. Cash them in if I don't return."

"If we don't return, you mean, Johnny . . ."

With a glance behind him to the closed door, he took out a round brass implement; a circle of letters wound about each other, an alphabet encompassing another of the same. He drew me to the window, to the moonlight through the green-house glass, and placed the piece in my hand. "Listen well, Asia. This is cipher. I want you to know it."

He rolled the object back and forth gently in my hand. "The alphabet, you see, how simple and wound fine into the piece it is? Every letter is in order, but the one just beneath it begins with the next. An 'A' becomes 'B' one column down."

"No, I don't see."

"Again, I'll show you again."

"Teach me later, after we've gone."

"Asia, you can't come."

My whole body was trembling now. "What are you saying?"

"Not now, Asia. I need you here. Playing this great role."

"Shut up, shut up!" I was shaking his shoulders. "This is the part I am to play? This is nothing!"

He held me against him. I heard his heart. "See, my love, there is always a key word. If I tell you the key word is 'MARRY,' you use that word so that each letter below the first will be the message. 'MARRY.' The letter 'M', look. Below 'M' is 'W'. That's the first letter of the encoded word. Do you understand?"

"No." I tried to break free. He restrained me. The letters danced along the circle as he held the object to my face.

"I'll send you a key word and the message, you'll encode it and send it on."

"Why must I know this?"

"So I can communicate with you."

"About what, for God's sake, about what?"

"If I am summoned, you will reply."

"What a joke, my God, Johnny, what a paltry joke." I pushed him away.

"They will come to you and I'll be ready."

"Who are *they?* Devils? Crows?"

"Be quiet, Asia."

"You've enlisted at last, have you, John Booth?"

"You know I promised Mama I would not."

"There is more, isn't there."

"Yes," he murmured, his hand on mine. And again the moonlight struck the gleam of metal and the parade of letters.

"More beyond the sending of dispatches?"

"I am going into southern Maryland. Surrattsville, Port Tobacco, and down. I'll expect my orders."

"From here?" My voice was rising.

"My control sends from Canada, here and then to me. And you, my brave actress, will play a glorious role."

"In what play? In whose play? Not mine!"

"We mean to make a capture. Of a monkey king."

I slapped him hard across the face. He ignored the blow. He reached into his travel bag and removed a dead pigeon, the leather pouch intact. He drew out Gillian's message from the pouch. "I know where Hulbert is. I'll send men after him, and Gillian."

I couldn't speak for the bile in my throat.

"You must help me, Asia. They've given me this mission, this Godly mission. I can't fail."

I stared at the inert pile of feathers that was one of Gillian's carrier pigeons, his neck twisted, his eyes dulled.

"Lincoln won't be harmed, Asia. I swear it. He'll be a hostage and we'll force an end to this war."

"Get out of here."

"It's been four years, Asia. How many more have to die?"

"They make a fool of you, of your famous face and name. They use you! Get out!"

His hands were forcing my hands.

"Encode. A simple message, anything."

Round and round we twisted the thing. I remembered the alphabet and the lines the letters must follow. I found a word.

"H-O-M-E."

"Again, say it."

"Home."

"Good. Practice. Write it on paper. Make a grid and follow the letters." He turned away, his face set, knowing I will never betray Hulbert James. "The war would end soon, Asia. No more will die." And then, in our old tongue, familiar and beloved, he recited, *"I prithee, tell me what you think of me."* I remembered the little boy I dared to jump off the roof of Father's house, the child I was meant to be.

"That you do think you are not what you are," I answered.

"If I think so, I think the same of you," Johnny Booth said.

"And then think you are right; I am not what I am," he added and pulled a sheaf of papers from his coat. "Hide these. If something happens to me . . ."

"My God, what are they?"

He held two more pages out to me. "The mission, the 'enterprise' and our reasons."

"Go!"

"When I get to Richmond, I'll send for you."

"Right. Damn you. *I would you were as I would have you be*," I said, my voice low and hard.

"Do you remember, Asia, Father's story of the Queen's man who grieved over a great wrong to England but could do nothing?"

"Yes, he was a mute. Father would play him by waving his hands in the language of signs and we would try to understand what he was saying."

"I am that man, but I am not mute," my brother said.

"Take me away, now. We'll stay on the farm forever."

"It's too late," he said, leaving me there with the

scent of his Switch-Bay cologne still in the air. My hand trembled as I held a paper to the lamp. It was enciphered. John Booth provided the key in clear script at the top, as though he knew it was to fall to me. As if he knew. I cursed the pages.

But I am ashamed to say I labored at the ciphers through the night.

"Here provided are the plans for—" what was the word?—"the detention of O.V.V."

Jesus, he must mean Lincoln, I thought. The rest was in open script, not encoded. "For the purpose of making hostage until Confederate victory achieved. The loyal Marylanders of the Route and signal line, John Wilkes Booth, David Herold, George Atzerodt, Lewis Paine and John Surratt." The last name was blurred by blots of ink and folded paper. I might have made it out, if I tried. I didn't want to know more.

I reached for a candle, moving the pages toward the flame. My hand stopped. Instead, I prayed for tomorrow and a new moon, faithless but full. And I stayed awake, hoping it was all a dream.

With the first speck of dawn, I hid his papers well in the house; the most secret in a place only I knew. The oil deeds, I stuffed in a carved rosewood box I kept under the stairwell. Ramblings, I told myself, the unkempt stutters of a mind on fire. He was only delivering quinine to the sick and dying, his famous face giving him free passage through the lines. It was only a new game on a new stage.

• • •

Soon it was habit. I met the messenger at the window of my husband's house in the heart of night, a tall man with a hat pulled low; a double rapping announcing his presence. "For Dr. Booth," he said, always in half shadow, yet a voice I thought I knew. My husband slept soundly as the dead and conducted our household with an apathy my brother well understood.

"For Dr. Booth," the messenger said and handed me the dispatch and a bag of quinine powder.

"Yes."

"You'll encipher?"

I did not answer, but held out my hand.

"God save the South," he said. "And the Enterprise."

"Go away."

As the messenger mounted his horse and sped off down the cobblestones, a rattling in my head began as I decoded the cipher, then plunged the dispatch and the quinine into the fresh dirt made ready near a stunted lilac bush.

I wrote, "Come Retribution." My God. And still I doubted. I watched from the window as another man retrieved the dispatch and the powder, knowing there would be more men at the window, more nights like these—all the while longing for all our childhood summers when we dreamed our-selves safe.

I splashed my face with rosewater and slipped

into bed beside my sleeping husband. I fell somewhere that was not sleep.

I heard the clink of glasses, the splash of liquid. They were gathered in a great dining hall, smoke from their inferior cigars purpling the air, a drone of English and southern accents. I was behind a heavy-hung damask drape. I was small and male with large, narrow feet. I saw a menu before one of them. "The Saint Lawrence Hall Hotel, Montreal," it read.

They spoke of the end of the world as they knew it, stuffing their mouths with squab, grease dappling their chins. One would have thought they were at a rowdy game of cards.

They spoke freely, did not dance about the subject or mutter in code.

"What of abduction?" asked an Englishman or a Canadian, I couldn't be sure. Another answered in a low drawl, a seeming bumpkin save for the clipped, clear voice and well-tooled manner.

"A dead end, sir, by God. It has been thwarted time and time again. And may I sample a bit of that fine brandy, as we in the South are forced to drink a sort of mule urine that passes for the same?"

"Of course, Mr. Thompson, drink away. Why did the abductions fail?"

"Each time they believed Old Abe to be present, a trick or an accident occurred. Who knows which?"

"I expect we might be so. It has all gone awry. A balding man in a heavy sweat leans heavily on the table. Please, the brandy?"

"Damn the brandy, Cleary. What is left, then?"

"If the White House bomber fails, God forbid, then we go to the others."

"The operatives, sir, the actor, Booth among them, are ready to strike in earnest."

"Booth is a fool."

"He's our fool."

"Fancies himself a savior."

"If all else fails, let him have his fun."

"And, so you desire endorsement, Thompson?"

"Yes, sir. President Davis has endorsed, as has Secretary Benjamin."

"We will deny any knowledge of you."

"Yes."

"And, as such, if you return here, you will be hanged."

"Yes, hanged, oh, God. For the good of our Confederacy, even that."

"Her majesty is in complete ignorance, and will evermore remain so."

"Of course."

"How and where will they flee?"

They were batting the cabal back and forth as though they play at croquet.

"To Richmond, of course, with the hostage."

"Through, where?"

"Southern Maryland?"

"The ragged outback hung with coon pelts?"

"The same."

"Protection of the operatives in escaping. You will see to that?"

"Of course," Thompson said. "We are grateful."

"We need your cotton, my man."

"Booth, then?"

"Yes."

Unable to swallow for the bile rising in my throat, the burn of the bile, I puked soundlessly. A bit seeped under the drape. A guard moved to the curtain and seized me by the arm.

"Alden?"

"Sir." My name was Alden.

"Alden, Jesus!"

"Who in God's name is that?" Thompson asks.

"My mute, my scholar mute, my transcriber, my witness. My fool now." The leader replies.

I opened my mouth to speak but cannot make a sound.

I was taken away.

They poured water down my throat, more water than any human could drink.

They didn't need to strangle me. I was dying fast, gagging and fading.

What thou see'st when thou dost wake,
Do it for thy true-love take;
Love and languish for his sake . . .
When thou wak'st, is it thy dear?
Wake when some vile thing is near . . .
  A Midsummer Night's Dream
  by William Shakespeare

24

April 15, 1865

I was choking.

"Swallow it, Asia. Swallow the brandy. Wake up, dear, try." I tried to open my eyes. The light was blinding. Under me, I felt soft goose down. Oh, Jesus, I was in my bed, in my room, with a man's face pressed to mine.

"Can you see now?" he asked. His hands were soft and gentle as he stroked my temple, all the while holding a cloth to the side of my head.

"Who are you?" I whispered.

"It's Dr. Miller, Asia. They sent for me. You fell and hit your head. Do you remember?"

I remembered.

"Hurry on, Doctor, wake her fully," a rough voice commanded, moving into view. It was my captor, Martin. Behind him was Gillian. She reached past him for my hand. I felt her strong fingers and held them tightly.

I forced my eyes shut. "I was there, Gillie and so were you and Mama and Father and Joh—"

"Shhh, dear, stay calm," Dr. Miller said sharply.

"Home. There were fires, horses were dying, my brother—"

"What in hell is she saying?" Martin demanded.

"She's regaining consciousness. The wound is not serious, give her time," Dr. Miller said.

"I don't have time, I need to question her!" Martin moved straight into my view. "Sit her up, I'm starting now."

I sat up slowly, dizzy from my fall and the visions upon visions. I didn't need Martin's hard hand behind my back. "How long have I been this way?"

"Hours, they say, dear," said Doctor Miller. "Thank God they reached me."

Martin and the Doctor pulled me to the corner of the bed.

"I'll move on my own," I said to Martin, only half-roused, with a frightful pain in my head. As I wobbled to my feet, Dr. Miller pressed a poultice to my head. "The bleeding has stopped. The swelling will go down."

"Clear the room," Martin ordered.

"I'm not leaving her," said Gillian.

Dr. Miller took her arm. "This is not the time to be uppity, Gillian, obey the good man's command."

"Isn't a good man here that I can see," she muttered.

"Put her below," said Martin to the soldier guarding the door. "Doctor, you've answered all my questions. You're free to go."

Dr. Miller bowed slightly. "I'll stay, and pray for you, Asia," he said.

The door of the room flew open, nearly knocking down the guard. Martin held me and pushed Gillian and Dr. Miller to the floor. Both Martin and the guard drew their guns and crouched, aiming at the door. As if charging through a squall, a man in civilian clothes materialized in the entryway. His hard-set glower marred an otherwise fine-boned face.

"Stand down," he said.

He was tall with skin the color of teak. With guns still trained on him he strode to Martin and thrust a badge past the weapon.

"Detective Norder from Washington City, Baker's force. I'll take it from here."

"On whose authority?"

"The Secretary of War." He produced a document from his jacket.

There were more voices from the street. I imagined rabid faces at the windows, men and women in a fierce heat. The detective wheeled around. "I want the perimeters cleared now. Understand?"

"I don't take orders from a high-yellow porch monkey," the guard-soldier muttered.

"Shut it, Private," Martin said.

The detective didn't flinch; instead he took a

telegram from his coat and handed it to Martin.

"Oh, my Christ," Martin moaned, passing the paper to the guard. Martin grabbed my arm, flattening my palm against his jacket. "Stinking initials are tattooed right here." Martin gripped me harder. "Did he put that brand on you?"

"I did it. When we were children," I said, hearing the rustle of a breeze by the pond and smelling summer in the reeds.

There was silence and a shifting of booted feet.

"They'll bag him sure, just like prey in the tall grass." Martin trained his gun on me. Gillian pushed past the doctor.

The detective lowered Martin's gun. "Do the same," he ordered the guard. "She's no good to us dead."

"Could have fooled me," the guard replied. "She's a liar sure."

"There will be justice," the detective said, looking straight at me. And to Martin he added, "Sergeant Conger's men are going into Maryland. You're to take a detail and follow."

"What about her?"

"I'll handle it." The detective fairly spat the words as though mouthing a curse.

Then, there was quiet. I felt the damp of my body through my morning gown. The detective spoke to me, to us all. "The President—" he caught his breath—"died this morning."

"Dear God in heaven," Gillian said, falling to her

knees. Dr. Miller grasped the arm of a chair, still as stone.

The detective stared ahead. Tears rolled down his face. He did not blink or move his hands to wipe them away. I was weeping too, quick gulps of air and a pain that nearly strangled me.

There was a ruckus in the hall.

"My wife will tell you who I am!" My husband was dragged into the room and thrown with his hands bound at my feet.

"We found these on him," a soldier said, thrusting papers at the detective.

"They're insane. All the Booths are mad!"

"Quiet, now!" The detective turned to me.

"Is that your husband?"

"Yes."

"I'm innocent," he shouted. "I'm a Lincoln man, I, oh, Christ, I own the Walnut Theatre, I . . ."

"Shut the fuck up," Martin ordered.

"He was crawling through the wine cellar, sir," a soldier said.

"Brave man to leave you here, lady," the detective said.

"Are you going to show me those papers?" Martin asked him.

"Deeds, nothing more," the detective answered. He held out the papers. Clearly embossed at the top were the words "Oil Shares. Pennsylvania Stock."

"He left them in my house? Jesus Christ!" He whimpered.

Martin nudged my husband with his boot. "Get him out of here."

"I am a Union man, sir, not a Rebel traitor!" cried my husband, his face the color of spent ash. "I had nothing to do with this evil!"

"Woman, is there more?" the detective said. "To deny or hide is treason!"

"No, sir, that is all."

Let them believe this, I prayed.

"Swear, woman, or swear your life away," Martin said, his hand raised up as though to strike me.

"She said that's all," the detective said this quietly. All turned and stared at him. A limp-jawed soldier spat on the floor.

"Why, oh lord, why must we listen to a nigger?"

My husband started to cry.

"It is all a terrible mistake," I said to him. "You'll see."

"Take him away," the detective ordered.

My husband moaned. "They are all Iago's, these Booths, and mad. I want no part of them!" The theatrical reference was lost on them. And Desdemona died at the hands of a Moor. Was that to be my fate?

I was confined to my bedroom. Gillian was allowed to remain. The soldiers rummaged through my dressers ripping my fine lace night-clothes and under-things, never speaking as they stomped about the room pulling papers from drawers, sweeping my combs and brushes from the nightstand. And finally, in the last drawer in my mahogany dresser—

"This yours, or his?" the soldier said, holding up a boldly checkered jacket and nankeen pants, too small for my husband. They were wrapped in tissue, tied with a ribbon. And in a small, silken case was the remains of a small cigar.

"Yours?"

"Yes."

"Does he leave his clothes here?"

"No."

"How often?"

"Never."

"What else?"

"Nothing. Nothing else. They're mine."

"Then smoke it," the soldier said, thrusting the thing in my mouth and striking a match.

Trembling, I took a puff, and then another, fighting not to heave or choke. *Little man,* I thought, *little fighting actor man.*

The detective watched silently, his eyes moving from my face to my possessions growing in piles all throughout the room.

I snuffed out the cigar stub, and reached toward a candle burning low on my desk. Shakespeare's words rattled in my brain.

"With trial-fire touch me his finger-end, if he be chaste, the flame will back descend." I moved my finger into the flame. *"And turn him to no pain;*

but if he start, it is the flesh of a corrupted heart." My hand jerked back. I was burned. "Help us, Daddy." The quiet voice was mine.

"Her father is—?" the detective asked.

"Gone," I answered.

"Dead as a doorstop," Gillian said.

O, banish me my lord, but kill me not! . . .
Othello by William Shakespeare

25

I grabbed her by the sleeve and held her against me. "Go to Hulbert," I whispered. "Why should you pay for this, this monstrous mistake?"

"Never."

"Leave me!" I pleaded.

"You are as good as my flesh," she whispered back. "I stay, Asia."

Gillian touched my face, her own hard and angry.

"I'm putting this woman to bed, if that passes fair with you, sir," she said to the detective waiting in the corner of the room, watching our every move but saying nothing. A soldier poked his head in the door and saluted him.

"Here's a right proper duty for you, Detective. It's a damn shame you can't be chasing Booth, boy. Stuck here, you are with that darky and her mistress. Here mammy, come on now," he called to Gillian. "I'll cakewalk you downtown."

"Don't you ever speak to her like that," I said.

"Oh, saucy, ain't we?"

"You heard her," said the detective.

I hugged Gillian to me.

The soldier gripped his holstered gun. "I must be in hell."

Gillian followed him.

"They won't hurt her," the detective said, as the soldier's voice echoed down the hall, singing.

"Charlotte town is burning down, goodbye, goodbye. Charlotte town is burning down, goodbye Liza Jane."

"Please, sir, may I go to my bed?" I asked the detective. I rose, and realized this was foolish.

My head lightened and I couldn't steady my feet. He caught me, lifting me into the air. There was about him a smell of lemon soap, a strange, sweet comfort amid my terror. He carried me up the stairs and placed me on my bed.

"Even here?" I was horrified at this invasion. "Am I allowed no privacy?"

"You are not."

"May Gillian attend me?"

"Not now."

I was in the keep of this stranger.

"Your colored girl will be allowed to help you," he said.

"For shame, boy, for shame," I imagined Gillian saying though she was not in the room.

"I am to not leave your side." He measured his words as though firing them at me.

"Everywhere?"

"What do you think? And this is not a question. I don't care what you think."

With this, he stepped right in front of me. A knife hung low on his belt.

And where would I run if I could?

I closed my eyes; my mind tumbled easily to another place with sounds and lights, as though they were before my eyes.

There was a campfire. A soldier knelt on the ground. Another stood over him wearing the stripes of an officer. He was raging mad, rising up and thudding his boot heels down on the ground.

"You lick-spittle fuck! How did you lose her?"

"She just up and skee-dadddled, Sergeant. Like smoke she was, rising from the watch fire, taking another shape and she was gone, I swear it."

"Do you know the penalty for that, fool?"

"Drummed out, sure."

"Are you ill, man? A spy don't come easy down the pike like some vagrant nigger. You are in the shit, brother."

"Here's the God's truth, Sergeant, before you stretch my neck. She was eating the corn bread I gave her and looking up at me with those mooning black eyes. Then she evaporated like she never was. Am I supposed to swing for that?" The soldier heaves a sob.

"Maybe she's yonder in the tree. Maybe you were sleeping off the rot gut you assholes swill. You'd best pray you find her."

"I shot all over them trees, sir, a possum come down like a pebble, but no woman did fall out."

"You are in it, brother. You are in it."

I cheered my imagined flight silently of course; as the woman spy who secreted dispatches in her petticoats and carried a razor in her boots.

The detective couldn't help but see the near-smile that flitted across my face. He shifted his weight, leaning imperceptibly toward me. I feared he would spring and tear me to pieces. His eyes never left me.

I had not known a mulatto in authority before, though I knew them to hold such posts in Washington City. I prayed he was a different sort, a man with shadows in his eyes but not an evil man. I envied him, drawn with anger at my side. Envied him his right to move about, as I could not.

"All the Negroes' colors are set in the skin before birth," Gillian said. "The dark ones are dray horses in the womb of the woman and if lighter they come into this life, they got a brick load of trouble. Master just can't hitch them to a plow or rub them raw in the fields, as he is in part looking at himself."

"Are you speaking to me?" The detective asked as if he had heard my thoughts. His voice was low and cold like winter wind.

"No, Detective."

"You'll come to no harm as long as you don't try to escape. Those are orders."

"What's your name?"

He seemed affronted by this question, then curtly replied, "Detective Rollie Norder," and as an afterthought, "born to a freedman."

"I'm sure that was hard won," I said.

"What do you know of such things?"

"Very little, sir," I said, thinking of Hulbert James and the mission he had imposed on himself.

I remembered what Hulbert told me as I dozed in his keep one storm-socked night. "Mr. Lincoln's emancipation don't help my people one whit."

"Why not, Mr. Hulbert James?"

"It's only for those still-bound, girl. I got me hundreds of them what the catchers want. And the money that comes with the bounty, that's what moves them."

"I am ignorant then."

"Didn't say that. Just white as a tablecloth," Hulbert said.

"Look at me!" The detective ordered.

Once again I feared he would tear me to pieces.

"Am I to die in your keep?"

"Not if you don't try to escape."

"You can trust that I will not try to escape, Detective. I am with child."

"Alright, then." He seemed quieted by my admission. "I could have hunted down Booth. I should have been on that detail. I could flush him out, but I'm here," he said.

"We're both trapped, aren't we, sir?"

I went to my bed, fully dressed, the bones of my corset stabbing my ribs. I pulled open my stays, holding the cover to my chin. Had his eyes been averted? I was so weary. It mattered not, this modesty of mine. The room darkened as night approached. My father's face was before me.

"He has killed, Asia. Shame be upon us. I do believe my heart shall break now."

"Not yet, Daddy. He cannot have killed."

"A trial, then, daughter?"

"I'm not ready, I swear it."

"Look deeper, daughter."

"What will I see or hear?"

"A howling and a chewing of wet fur."

"What will I see, damn it!"

"Look in the mirror."

"Not yet."

"Very well."

I touched the window. It was, of course, without a single shape in the glass. I thought to break it with my fist. I looked to the detective. The thought was folly.

"I am shackled here," I said to him. "Will next come the lash?"

"Don't be a fool," he told me.

He paced close to me as though tethered himself. The detective was a mute witness to my contorted half-sleep. Some time later, hours, many hours later—

"Your husband is a coward," he said.

"What will happen to him?"

"He'll be held in the Old Capital Prison and interrogated."

"He knows nothing."

"Do you?"

I had no words.

"Do you? You won't live to see your baby!"

"Leave me alone!"

"He killed the best man that ever lived." There were tears in his eyes.

"Lincoln was a great, good man. I am grief struck for all of us."

"What do you know, here in this house with that colored woman emptying your slops?"

"Gillian is a free woman. She could leave at any time. She helped to raise us."

"A slave is a slave."

I tried to meet his eyes but he would not look at me. "Thank you, Detective."

"For what?"

"For helping me earlier."

"I didn't do anything."

"My mistake," I said.

I turned over and rested my head on the pillow, my arms bared as the cover fell. "My brother is not a killer."

"Go to sleep," the detective said. "Head wounds don't heal on their own."

I turned my head to the wall and closed my eyes.

I heard raucous laughter and applause.

I saw him.

Thou basest thing, avoid hence, from my sight.
Cymbeline by William Shakespeare

26

His face was in shadow. He was inching through a narrow space, perspiring heavily. He wore a black frock coat. There was a sound of muffled voices. A play was in progress. He mouthed the lines as he crawled through the darkness.

"Not heir to the fortune, Mr. Trenchard." Gaslights from the floor above gave faint illumination through cracks in the wood. There were short bursts of laughter. And still he crawled.

"Yes, Ma, the nasty beast," an actress whined.

"Beast, beast, almost, almost," he said, crawling toward a light at the end of the passage.

He came upon two people in an embrace: a Union soldier and a small man in a straw hat with rouged cheeks and long, blonde hair. The soldier's pants were around his knees. He drew his gun.

"It's safe, sweet William. He's a friend," the small man said, smiling like a skittish maiden.

"Good evening Josey," the black-frocked man said.

"Good evening to you, dear," the small man replied.

The soldier wove unsteadily, still holding his gun, all the while trying to close his pants.

"I said, he's a friend, William."

"If you say so." The soldier grunted. "Pass by then, mister."

"Thank you." The man moved quickly now. The voices of the actors grew louder as he emerged from the passage. He was in a theatre now, just behind the rows of box seats. There were whispers of recognition, a few swoons. He inched along; brushing the naked shoulders of silken gowned women as he passed.

"As if I weren't as fancy as that ragged pelt you call a frock?" an actor shouted from the stage.

The audience tittered.

"Don't know the manners of good society, eh?" another actor retorted. The man slipped past an empty chair outside a theatre box.

"Guess I know enough to turn you inside out, old gal!"

He opened the door and stepped inside. President Lincoln leaned forward, smiling broadly. His long, weathered face was weary; his long, thin body was folded into a rocking chair. He was holding the hand of his wife. Plump and pink in a full bonnet with rose-colored flowers pinched at her cheeks, she smiled up at him like a new maiden.

"You sockdologizing old man trap!" an actor yelled. The audience roared with laughter.

The man behind Lincoln raised a derringer and fired at the back of Lincoln's head. There were puffs of smoke and silence as all were frozen for an instant.

Suddenly, the President's wife shrieked at the top of her voice.

The shooter swung low like a wild animal, stabbing at a man as he dodged in front of him. He vaulted over the theatre box and leapt into the air. "*Sic Semper Tyrannus!*"

"Who are you?" I cried to the shadow killer that had no face.

The picture blurred and faded.

"Why can't I see you?" I screamed. All was hazy, then.

"Why?" I said again. "Why can't I see you?"

"You are not supposed to just yet," a man answered from behind me as he wrapped a rope around my neck. "How would the noose fit this pretty flesh?"

He held me to the bed, covering my mouth. I could not move or cry out.

"Do you fight? I bet you do. My wife never makes a sound." He reeked of alcohol. The rope tightened. I kicked hard against him. I was no match. He raised my gown, his hand moving up my bare leg.

"Get out." It was Detective Norder's voice. I saw him out of the corner of my eye. His gun was drawn.

"She wants it, she said so," the soldier said.

"No!" I screamed.

"If you come near her again, I'll kill you," Norder said.

The soldier moved toward the door. "She deserves worse."

"Turn around." Norder pushed the gun into the soldier's back. "Move." He backed him to the door. "Let's go."

I heard the bolt snap shut behind them. I fell back on the bed.

Soon, Norder came back.

"Did he hurt you?"

"No."

"I was summoned to get dispatches while you slept. It won't happen again. Sit up, please." He spoke softly.

He showed me a sheaf of dispatches. "They've got witness statements now. There is no doubt. They saw your brother jump from the President's box onto the stage."

I knew, I saw. I was silent. With closed eyes, I asked, "How did it happen?"

"He shot the President in the head."

My body weakened.

"From the back. Lincoln never saw the coward's face."

"Did the President suffer?"

"He never woke."

I felt a sharp pain in my stomach. I prayed I was not losing the child.

"Secretary Seward was stabbed by one of Booth's accomplices. There was a massacre at his house. He may not live."

"My brother could not kill a man."

"He did and he will hang. If he was my kin, I'd be ashamed to my grave."

"If he did this thing, Detective, I will be as you say."

"There's no 'if' now."

"Maybe." I faced him straight on. "Maybe it was not to end this way!"

"What are you talking about?"

"Maybe, it was a mistake!"

He grasped my shoulders, an invasion of my modesty he had never breached. His breath was on my face; his eyes bored into mine.

"A mistake? A President is killed by mistake?" I tried to pull free. He tightened his hold. "What are you saying?"

"Suppose it was a, a plan gone awry. Just suppose they—"

He pulled me to the table. "Is this fantasy, excuses, delusion, what? What do you know?"

The shutters rattled as thunder sounded. A sharp wind doused the candles. We were in the darkness, body to body. I heard his ragged breathing as he heard mine. I believe I fainted.

Through the heavy scrub, by the low light of a lantern, a band of men waited in the shadows. He was wearing a heavy, black topcoat, open at the front. A pair of pistols was visible just inside.

"Again . . . tall hat, whistle once, that was the

signal. How could we go so wrong?" he said, his voice near a sob.

Another man answered, a giant with no clear features. "I got there didn't I? It ain't my fault we trussed up the wrong man, Captain!"

"Unless the monkey man did shrink down to a beaver," a high, singsong voice answered from the shadows.

"Dumb greaser, you blew it!" the giant shot back.

"Silence! It was not the President's carriage," the heavy-coated man said, the leader. "We'll try again. If not, we weigh options."

"Kill him, you mean?" the small man asked.

"Who asked you to be our executioner, Captain? I'm flat out of this now."

Another man gave voice. He was at a crouch, but appeared lithe and young. "You'll all take the oath or you don't leave," he said.

"Jesus, I'm sick here. It is murder you are talking." This whisper came from a man behind a live-oak tree.

"Mike," the leader asked, "at Bull Run, how many of privates did you kill?"

"Ten at least," was the answer, "at least that I could see hit the ground."

"So what warrior would not leap at the chance to down the General?" the leader asked.

"You told me it was six Yanks, Mike," the crouching man said.

"You shut it," Mike answered.

"Place your hands in mine, and swear—" the leader said.

"Jeeesus!" the child man whimpered. The lantern flickered and went out.

Another lamp flashed before my eyes.

"Jeeeesus, look at this will you!" The soldiers barged into my bedroom, bringing brightly lit lamps with them. The detective moved quickly away from me.

One soldier held an elaborate brocade cape, the back in tatters; the other lugged a decorated steamer trunk. One of them chopped at the lock with an axe, smashing the front as broken wood covered the floor. They yanked out the contents.

"His name is on some, look." A soldier thrust a cape at the detective, with the name "J. W. Booth" clearly written on a hanging label.

"Yeah? So what?" The detective said. "It proves nothing. Get back to your duty."

"You're not my commander."

"Go. Now."

"Yes, sir, Mr. Negro, yes sir." In parting they chopped the trunk to pieces. Wooden swords, tragedy masks, and an ermine cape littered the floor.

I looked at the broken sword.

Once I taught him to fence. I was good at it. We were young.

"*En garde*! Johnny. Now move to the side, and advance." My brother tried to follow me and was clumsy. "Look, the tree there? That is the foe,

Johnny. Slow now, as a dance. Move, thrust, move, sideways, advance." He stumbled, his sword flew in the air and he fell into the tree.

"Middling, boy. Watch and learn." I swept across the grass, my hand poised in the air. "I am the king's follower and will rid him of this foe!" I plunged the sword tip into the tree. "Ha! He is stabbed in the heart. Now, you."

Johnny sighed.

"Next, we shoot." I held up a gun.

"Where did you get it?" he asked.

"It's Father's. You see that?" I said, pointing to an empty brandy bottle atop the fence. I handed him the weapon.

He pointed the gun and pulled the trigger.

I didn't realize I held the sword in my hand. The detective took it from me.

"This is where nightmares live, Detective. Not in craven things that lurked behind bushes, but in the face of my mistakes."

Rain was falling again.

"You should eat," Norder said.

I looked up from my full plate. "I cannot."

"For the child," he said.

"I don't need advice from you. And I don't need to be kept like this either. It's indecent!"

"You're looked after at least and not thrown to a mob. Your other brothers have been arrested."

"They haven't seen him since he was a child.

Please God, don't tell me my mother was arrested as well?"

"She was not, but there is a watch on her."

"I need her and she needs me."

"Your mother would not be allowed to travel."

"Then we'll meet in hell!"

"He killed a great, good man, and for that we will all pay, woman." He handed me a bowl of soup and a spoon. "Eat," he ordered.

I obeyed him. He leaned back in his chair and took an easy tone. I was disquieted by this softness. "The first time I saw your brother on the stage," he said, "I'd never seen anything so accomplished. I went for two nights running. He played Hamlet. It cost me a week's pay."

I pictured the detective in the audience, with another face, one not so fixed and shrouded.

"Where might he have gone?" he asked.

"I've told you, I don't know."

"I tracked a man once, a Rebel spy. Hounds cornered him, and then vultures got what was left. Didn't leave much for me, or the hangman. His own kin didn't recognize him," he said, his eyes never shifting from my face. "Hangman was kind of glad though. He spent the day napping and rolling marbles through the trap. Where would your brother seek safety and with whom?"

"Stop it, please, stop it."

"Where?"

"I swear I don't know."

"On the life of your unborn child?"

"Yes."

I leaned back in the chair. "Please, let me be in quiet. Please, Detective."

"I will, for now," he said.

I heard a song.

"Molly would not marry me, neither would she let me be." A small man with the face of an errant schoolboy was singing, holding a haggard man around the waist, dragging him along.

"Fetch her coffee, fetch her tea—just a little farther, Captain."

"I feel no pain, Davey, except for those I left behind."

"You did good, Cap. You said it yourself."

"Did I?"

"You followed orders, Captain. That is the brave truth."

"So I did. Please don't let me fall, Davey."

"I won't Cap."

The voices faded.

I thought I heard the baying of hounds, or was it the wind in the eaves? I tried to force down the soup, and think of my baby inside me. And of other things: The portrait of the President that hung over our mantel. His gentle face and his huge, heavy-veined hand resting gently on the shoulder of his son.

My brother followed orders, as did I.

. . . I do care for something: but in my conscience,
sir, I do not care for you: if that be to care for
nothing, sir, I would it would make you invisible.
Twelfth Night by William Shakespeare

27

He placed a blanket over my shoulders. His touch was gentle. "It was cold in here," the detective said.

I sat stiff against my parlor chair, which had been embroidered by my mother when she was awaiting the birth of my brother. I wanted to speak with the detective, anything that might pass for human contact, even though his somber gaze rarely changed.

"I am called Asia," I said. "On a whim, I am told, of Father's. I'm named for the exotic continent."

"I've never been out of this country," he answered. I was grateful for those few words.

"Nor I. But if imaginings count, I've been to the moon and back—where all is peaceful and white."

His gaze softened. I was safe to continue, I believed. "Have you a wife, Detective?"

He flinched.

"I'm sorry if I've been unseemly, sir."

"She died last winter giving birth to our son."

"I'm sorry."

"She made fancy gowns for rich women. She got the childbed fever."

"Your son?"

"He survived."

I wanted to say more but the pain in his voice made me weak.

"I'm locking the door," he said. "I'll be back soon."

"Don't go, please, Detective."

"You'll be safe."

"It isn't that."

"What then?"

"I would like to talk, sir."

"About?"

"Talk to you. I find it—you—of value, sir."

"I said I have to check for dispatches," he said.

I looked out the window.

The street was empty save for a few soldiers posted about the house. I saw Norder below and my drunken assailant riding off with a scowl. His hands were tied to the pommel of his saddle. In front of him, a mounted soldier spurred his horse. I fixed my eyes on the shiny flank of the animal. The soldier spurred him in an easy rhythm. Kick, again, kick, again.

The horse was a deep chestnut brown and lathered, breathing hard, as was . . . my brother. I saw him clearly for the first time.

He cantered up to the guard station on the bridge.

"Good evening to you, sir," the sentry said.

"Good evening," my brother answered in a voice that was steady and calm. "May I pass?"

The sentry tilted a lantern toward his face. "Oh, yes, sir, Mr. Booth. I seen you on the stage just two nights back. You were great in the Apostle."

"The Apostate. The play was the Apostate."

"Right. I got the last ticket. I had to fight my brother for it. He—"

"Yes, yes, I'm indeed flattered." My brother held his hand to his leg. It was twisted in the stirrup. "Excuse me, I really must go now."

"But, it's late to pass, sir. Truth be told, I was off pissing when a Reb passed last week. They said they couldn't find me, no moon that night."

"Christ, man," my brother said, looking behind him, "let me pass now."

"Where you headed, then?"

"Beantown and thank you, sir. I have business there. Urgent business."

The guard rambled on. "Once a secesh whore ran her hands up my leg and says to let her pass. I took the letters off the bitch and read 'em while I was pissin'. They be coded. I know it. They went like this: 'Mama, send me some tooth powder down to Chantilly, so I can have a sweet mouth to face the bullet. Signed: Your son, Wesley.'"

My brother told hold of the sentry's arm. His own hand moved to grip his pistol. "Let me go, now."

"I knew the God damn guard who was here in my place," the sentry said. "Chicken-ass baby let them Rebels pass. What good are you if you can't spot the devil, even in the dark? I wasn't off with no whore then. I wasn't. I swear it!"

"I'm sure of it. Goodbye."

My brother went to a slow trot, wincing, as the pain was sharp and sharper.

"You want to bear witness to my fidelity at my post?" the guard called after him. "A famous man such as yourself?"

My brother spurred his horse into the darkness.

My own leg shook uncontrollably. A sharp pain shot through it. There was a knock on the door. I stood and limped to open it. "Who is there?"

"He says he's your pastor," the detective answered.

"Reverend Jessup come to call on you, Asia," Gillian called from behind the door.

I opened the door. Gillian's eyes held mine. I admitted a man in a long, brown coat, his face nearly covered by a woolen muffler.

"Reverend Jessup wishes to bring a letter from the congregation," Gillian said slowly. The detective stood behind the man in the coat, watching.

"As you have always been right good to our Gilllian," the man said, "I come to give you a prayer."

I knew the voice. "Thank you, Reverend."

"And because you've given food baskets and money to the poor of this place, we know there is no evil in your heart." He lowered his muffler.

I was trembling now as I beheld the raptor eyes of Hulbert James. "May I set?" he asked.

"Of course."

"We wish you to know we are here," he said.

Gillian's face was impassive.

"And we wish you to feel some small comfort as we are . . . all around you." He touched my hand. "As one young girl gave such comfort in the darkness as the hounds of hell passed him by. As one good soul helped a man long ago."

Hulbert James saw me covering his scent with urine, this I knew now. This I knew. "Thank you, Reverend. Thank you."

"Do you have scripture you wish me to recite?"

"You choose. Yes, please, Reverend."

"And Jacob was left alone and wrestled with an angel," he said.

"Until the break of day," I replied.

"But the hollow of Jacob's thigh was out of joint as he wrestled with him. The angel said . . ." He gripped my hands and pressed a tiny, sheathed knife into my palm. He continued in a gentle voice. "Let me go, for the day breaketh. And Jacob said, 'I will not let thee go except thou bless me.' "

"Except thou bless me," I said.

"Bless you, child."

I wept against the long brown coat of Gillian's husband, the tiny knife burning in my hand.

The detective watched the display without expression.

"May I show the Reverend out?" Gillian asked.

"Yes," he said.

The door closed behind them.

"I'm ill, Detective. I must have privacy to change my under-things." He unfolded my dressing screen. "May I have a basin of water?"

Behind the screen, I knelt, hiding the knife deep in the top of my high-laced boot.

"Take your time," he said.

"Thank you."

"Are you all right?" Norder asked.

"I don't know."

I did know. The waking visions were coming fast now.

John Booth was riding through a swamp, inching his way through brambles and mud. His voice was weak but Shakespeare's words were on his lips.

"Had you rather Caesar were living, and die all slaves than that Caesar were dead to live all free men?" His head lolled to one side. *"I did slay the beast for the good of Rome."*

I heaved into the basin. At once, Gillian was beside me, steadying me. When I finished, I spoke loud enough for the detective to hear me.

"So good of the Reverend to come to us." And then, I whispered, "Thank God he is near you."

"He forgives, Asia."

"Do you, Gillie?"

"You can answer me the *why* child. The why of Johnny's killing father Abraham. And if there ain't no answer, then you best turn your face away so I can never again see that boy looking at me out of your eyes." With that, she walked away.

"Dearest Mama," I wrote. I was allowed by the detective to write one letter. "I pray you are not without comfort. Not a moment goes by that I do not think of you. Gillian is with me. She says she would come to you if she could. I am in the keep of a good, quiet man so you must not worry for my safety. I love you, Mama. Don't be afraid. Your Asia."

"May I send this?" I asked the detective, showing him the letter.

"I'll see to it."

"Thank you, Detective Norder."

"Your brother is still at large."

"I see."

"They want you in Washington City. I'm to accompany you."

"For what?"

"Questioning."

"She can't go! She's ill!" Gillian hovered in the doorway, a hot kettle in her hand that she waved at the air like a weapon.

The soldier who had brought this news fairly danced with delight. "They're close on him now. It's just a matter of time."

"Then why take her?" Norder asked.

"For when they catch him, son. There's others in the mix. They'll be a trial. She can testify, then she can watch him swing."

"She'll need a doctor's okay," Norder said. "Travel might imperil her."

"Might what? Speak English," the soldier said.

"Go for Dr. Miller."

Later that day, I asked Norder to take me to my garden. "Might I lean on you, Detective? I must see my flowers."

He did not answer but offered his arm.

The flowers were blooming; larkspur and violets covered the ground. I pressed my face to their fragrance.

"What is it like to kill?" I asked him.

"What kind of a question is that?"

"What is it like?"

He turned away. "Easy at first," he said. "Too easy. If you don't see their eyes."

"That makes it different?"

"Of course." He knelt beside me. I could have stabbed him right then.

"There is a rush in your chest," he said. "You want to scream but you don't. If you see the bullet go in, it is sucked in, deep in the skin and doesn't bleed at first. And you don't look at the eyes." He rubbed his arm, wincing.

"Are you in pain?"

"I took a minnie ball at Vicksburg. It never healed properly. That's why I got this detail."

"You were a hero in battle, this I know."

He looked stunned. He looked away.

"I led a detail over a ridge. We didn't stop until we were stopped. That's all."

"I know you to be brave."

"Thank you."

"How do you bear the slurs, the ridicule?"

"I take another skin and don't hear them at all. I see through white eyes in those times, in most times."

"I have dreamed myself a man, sir, felt it even. Do you understand that?" I asked.

"Tend to the flowers if you need to, tend to them," he said.

"I'll tend to you, Detective, if that's alright. I have a balm that will soothe your arm."

In my room, I took a small pot of salve from my dresser. "My husband ridicules my remedies, but they work. Open your coat." He hesitated. "This will help, I promise."

He removed his jacket and rolled up his shirt-sleeve to reveal a badly scarred arm. I gently rubbed in the salve. His skin was puckered at the scar, an angry red line against his coffee skin. I was touching this angry man and was not embarrassed or for a moment afraid.

"It's cooling," he said. "It's cooling."

I don't know why I spoke next. "I wanted to be my brother. From the time we were children, to be him. Father wouldn't let me be an actress, so I slipped into my brother. I disappeared."

He was still as I continued to apply the balm. "I did not mind it, you see—becoming him. I did not mind it at all. That is my sin."

The detective buttoned his jacket. The sad, hard look returned. "He wasn't your pastor, was he? The man who came."

I didn't respond.

"I could see it in your colored woman's face."

"I've known him from childhood. He gave me a blood trust and I never betrayed it. Gillian loves him more than her life."

"Do you love your brother that much?"

"Is that what this is about? Another interrogation?"

"You tell me."

"Go to hell."

"I'm already there," he said.

"So sir, am I."

I made a decision then and there.

"I must use the privy. Surely I can be trusted to go alone?"

"Yes."

I pushed past him, down the hall and ducked into the nursery. I stared at the crib, my hand on my stomach.

"If you can hear me, my love, do not be ashamed of us. We were a family once and loved each other fiercely." I ran my hand along the baby quilt.

"Forgive me."

• • •

I climbed to the garret. It was close and warm. I locked the door, closed my eyes, and waited. Apple blossoms were falling to the ground—the white, snowy puffs, the bright green grass, and the stillness. My brother lay beneath a tree, his leg propped on a box. A dark new growth of stubble covered his face. A large man with gnarled hands moving as though forcing his bulk against a wind approached him.

"You gotta get on. I'm going up to town. It's the last day of the tobacco market. You got to leave now."

"Please let me stay a while longer," my brother said.

"Are you daft, you son-of-a-bitch? We never countenanced no killing. It was supposed to be a capture, that's all!"

My brother reached into his pocket and pulled out several shiny gold coins. He handed them to the man.

"I can't pick shit no more since the Yankees took my niggers." He grabbed the coins and bit down on one. "One hour you got. 'Til dark."

"I am grateful, sir."

My brother stood with difficulty, leaning on a wooden crutch. He hobbled a bit, then, fell heavily to the ground. He crawled toward a farmhouse, dragging his leg behind him.

"I am gone, sir," he recited.

I pulled the cover from a mirror in the corner of the room. My face was his face, as my hair was dirty and pulled straight back. *"I am gone, sir,"* I said to the man in the glass with a frock coat and high black boots. I knelt, feeling along boards below me. I found the loose one and pried it up. Inside rested a silver-handled pistol and bullets. I loaded the gun.

"I am gone, sir," I said. *"And anon, sir, I'll be with you again."* I aimed at the mirror, at him, at us. *"In a trice, Like to the old vice, Your need to sustain; Who, with dagger of lath, In his rage and his wrath, Cries, ah, ha! to the devil."* I cocked the trigger.

"Like a mad lad, Pare thy nails, dad; Adieu, good man devil," I said.

I fired. We disappeared in the shattered glass.

Someone was kicking down the door.

The detective rushed in, stopping short at the sight of me. Behind him was Hulbert James. Gillian pressed behind him. I turned the gun on myself.

"God Jesus!" Gillian cried.

"That ain't gonna make it right," Hulbert said softly.

"Give me the gun," the detective ordered.

"Listen to him, child." Gillian was crying.

"Don't weep for me, Gillie," I said evenly.

The detective held out his hand. "Please." I had never heard his voice so gentle. "Please."

"Will you tell the slave catchers about Hulbert James?" I asked.

"No."

"He loves her."

"Give me your hand," the detective said.

"What does it matter to you?"

"Is this an interrogation?" he asked. Something close to a smile crossed his mouth.

"No, Detective."

"You are not your brother. You did not kill the President."

"I don't remember."

"Yes, you do."

They waited. I waited. Did I want to die then? Did he? I thought I heard a baby cry far in the distance. I turned toward the sound.

"Let Johnny go, Asia, let him go," Gillian said.

There was an odor of black powder from the shot I had fired, acrid and burning.

I saw smoke crawling along the dirt floor of a shed. Broken furniture and bundles of dried tobacco leaves were piled in the corners. He coughed, wiping at his eyes. A piece of flaming straw flew through the air.

"Booth!" A man shouted. "Come out, it's over."

A burning timber crashed at his feet.

"Then let God so speed me . . ." His voice was strong and deep. *"For I love the name of honor more than I fear death."* He limped toward the door, a carbine in his hand.

"Booth! I've come from Philadelphia, from your sister!" It was Martin's voice. He'd found my brother.

John Booth stopped, rocking back and forth as fire burned through the dried tobacco and up the walls. He dropped the carbine and the crutch, staggering toward the door. "Asia!"

There was gunfire.

The barn burst into flames.

"Johnny!" I screamed.

Norder grabbed the gun from my hand.

"Alright now, baby, alright," Gillian said. Hulbert James and Gillian held me then.

"Go down the back stairs, man," the detective said and handed Hulbert the weapon. "There's no guard there now."

Hulbert pocketed the gun and slipped out the door. The detective helped me to my feet. "You didn't kill Lincoln," he said.

"I know," I replied.

I bless the time when my good falcon made her flight across Thy father's ground.
The Winter's Tale by William Shakespeare

28

His fingers probed deep inside me. "You appear to have some blood, Asia. Have you had much before?"

"No, just an occasional cramp and weakness," I answered.

"I must continue to examine her. It will be very delicate," Dr. Miller said to the detective as I lay in bed behind a screen.

"Go on, then. I'll wait," the detective said.

The doctor probed again. "Then it is not so abnormal. You're strong, so very strong," he said loudly. Dr. Miller leaned close to my face. His hands were on either side of my shoulders, pinning me to the bed. His voice was at a low whisper I could barely hear. "Thank you, Asia."

"For what?"

"Your help with the Enterprise."

I did not understand him at first.

"Your brother is alive. We've had word. He has been housed on the route and will try to make it to Richmond, to freedom."

"What?"

And then, I realized what he had just said.

"You?"

"How do you think the dispatches made it past the Yankees at this station?" He leaned closer, his face touching mine. "You are a heroine, my dear. You are owed much."

"My God."

I might have called for the detective, but did not. "Where is my brother?"

"He's on his way to Richmond. He's gone by way of southern Maryland. The route. You know the route as well as I do." He raised his voice. "Almost finished, my dear. You won't lose the child surely. There now, don't cry."

And again, he whispered. "Listen now. The nigger who watches you is to accompany you to Washington. On the way we'll kill him, replace him with our guard, and you will be free. If it is possible, you'll see your brother after that."

"When? When will this happen?" My mouth was dry.

"At nine o'clock tonight. It's been arranged. You'll need to secure the papers. Bring them with you."

"That's not possible."

"There are names, Asia. Yours among them."

"Yours too?"

"The whole Doctor's Line. We'll all hang if we are revealed. John Booth is waiting for you." The doctor took my hands and pressed them to his face. "God save the South."

He slowly drew the cover over my near-naked

body and said in a louder tone, "Yes, Asia, you seem well, just exhausted."

Dr. Miller backed out of the room, his eyes still on me, hard, watchful. "I will be back tonight with a proper document attesting to her condition, Detective. She is very frail, but she will bear the journey, poor child."

I lay in my bed clutching the cover around me.

Gillian came and went, bringing me broth to sip. The detective returned to his place at my side. I could not look at him. Tonight, he would be dead and I would be free.

Later, I walked slowly through the house touching the carved wood of the mantle, the lightness of the silken drapes as they came to rest on my fingers, moved by a breeze. The detective didn't speak. He simply walked where I walked, now and then stopping before a picture of my father and mother or a treasured family book.

"Where is your home?" I asked.

"Near the Washington Arsenal, where they'll hang the conspirators after the trial."

"How long will they keep me?"

"I don't know." He seemed very sad. "I'll be there, you know," he said.

"Mother of God, how did it come to this?"

He reached out his hand. His fingertips nearly touched my shoulder. "When I leave this duty, I will take my son to the grave of the President," the detective said.

"Does he look like you?"

"Dark, like his Mama. With her eyes."

"He'll welcome the sight of you, sir."

"I pray it is so," he answered.

This soft talk moved time only a fraction. We sat together. I waited.

It was nearly time. I moved as though hypnotized to the parlor, my travel bag in my hands. I looked at the hall clock with its molded face and hands. Almost nine.

There was a rapping on the door.

The detective turned to me.

"Are you ready?"

"Yes."

He went to the door.

"Who is there?"

"Doctor Miller and the night detail."

I could not look as he opened the door. As his hand reached the doorknob, I held tight to his arm. He stiffened.

"No!" I whispered to him. "Stop!"

"You have to go," he said. "You have to do this."

"Don't open it, please don't!" I said.

Dr. Miller stood before us, his hand on the arm of the stranger who accompanied him. A voice was raised. It was mine. I rushed at the doctor. "No, Detective! They mean to kill you!"

The detective pulled me back. In that instant the doctor pushed past us. The other man came into the room, his gun drawn. He pointed it at the detective.

"No!" I screamed as I pushed hard at the detective. He toppled forward. The bullet crashed into the wall.

I yanked the knife from my boot and stabbed the stranger in the hand. He screamed, dropped the gun and held me by the hair.

The doctor grabbed the gun and pointed at the detective.

"Stinking nigger!" he cried.

The stranger was pulling me across the floor. I kicked and clawed at him.

Before the doctor could fire, the detective did. The doctor fell, shot in the shoulder.

"Damn you," he screamed. "Asia! Damn you!"

Gillian leapt at the stranger, hitting him again and again with an ash bucket.

The stranger's hands were around my neck. He was choking me. His hands were like iron claws at my throat.

The detective clubbed him with the butt of his gun. He fell on me, his fingers flexed, his nails tearing my skin. The detective freed me from the man's grasp and dragged both men to their feet.

"You've betrayed us, Asia," the doctor said.

"Yes, I have!"

"Your brother will hear of this."

"No, he won't."

Gillian wrapped me in her arms. "God, Jesus," she said. "Help us all."

After the doctor and his accomplice were bound

and taken away by the night guard, the detective and I sat together.

"Thank you," he said. "Are you in pain?"

"Yes," I said to the man I could not bear to see die. "I don't care anymore what becomes of me, sir."

"I'm sorry to hear that. Morning is here. We'll soon go to the prison."

And in the dawn, as I fought sleep, as the gray became morning, I saw him. I saw my brother lying on the farmhouse porch, blood pooling under his head.

"Lift my hands for me," he said. "I can't feel them." A woman knelt and dabbed at his mouth with cloth. "Useless, useless," he said, as his hands hung limp. "Tell Mama and my sister I did what I thought best," my brother said. "Tell them I died for my country." Tears ran down his cheeks.

I went to the window. A group of people were forming at the edge of the street, holding papers and pointing toward the house.

Gillian walked slowly into the room. She held out her arms to me.

"Captured?" I said to the detective.

"Yes."

"Dead?"

"Yes."

I turned my face to the wall.

"What of my husband?"

"Maybe he won't come back."

"And me?"

"You knew nothing."

"Go to the nursery," I said. "In the hollow bed-post of the crib you'll find papers. It's what they were looking for."

A long while later, he came back, bearing the documents.

"Like I said, you knew nothing," he told me.

Soon he was leaving. I was in the garden. From my overall pocket, I took a small pouch of herbs and handed it to him.

"If ever your son is ill with croup or ailments of the chest . . ."

"Thank you."

He picked up his bag and walked to his horse. "Goodbye, Asia." It was the first time he spoke my name.

I dug and dug in the dirt until my hands went numb; in the black soft dirt very like that of the farm when a long ago April found us young and safe.

Adieu good man devil . . .
   Twelfth Night by William Shakespeare

29

April 15, 1866
One year later

"She is kin to the devil!" strangers raged often and loudly. In consequence and to make his life easier, my husband insisted we leave our country for England, where it is rumored the sun smirks like a half-wit in a gray sky. He permitted me little movement and offered daily reminders—the suppers he downed alone, the gaping silences, the closed bedroom door—of my disgrace. Perhaps out of pity, he allowed me to go home one last time.

"I'll come back for you at dusk," he said, climbing into the black coach that brought me to the edge of the meadow just across from our old house.

"No later, Asia, do you hear?" My husband rapped the driver's shoulder sharply with the tip of his walking stick, as if commanding the poor man to pull the thing himself.

"He is not a dray horse, Mr. Clarke," I murmured.

"What?"

"Nothing," I said. "Nothing."

"Don't trouble anyone," he called to me.

"I won't."

"Dusk, then? You'll meet me, Asia?"

"Yes." I avoided his eyes. "Thank you for this."

"Right," he said, "don't trouble anyone." He slumped against the red leather seat of the black coach, his mouth set tight as a new-caught clam. The crack and groan of wheels on rocks told me he was leaving.

"You need to call up love, girl," my beloved Gillian might have told me. *Hard to do that,* I thought, *with a heart stone that dares me draw a proper breath.* "Hunt down memory, Asia." I heard her voice, just like that. "That's why you are here."

A gust of moist air thick with the scent of wild lilacs lifted my hair and teased my face. I ran through the tall tick-weed; the scratch of it against my legs was familiar. A wide-winged yellow butterfly soared overhead. I ran past oaks and barrel-thick pines—fast and faster now. There lay the meadow spotted with cornflower and foxglove.

"My God," I said. "I am home."

Shadows edged over the door of my father's house. I crept closer, my heart sinking. "It's broken, Dad. They've dashed your beautiful windows to pieces and the rhyming balcony sags low like it might tumble away," I whispered. I stood there in front of the ruin for a long time, summoning up the mettle to go inside. I stepped up to the porch where many times Johnny and I hid from the wizard of dusk—the gray, sightless being who kept the moon in a gold watch, we believed—immense and terrifying. I rapped lightly on the door.

"Declare yourself." It was a woman's voice.

"A visitor," I said.

"And your name would be?"

"I'm, I'm—" I pulled a name out of the air—"Carrie Lawton."

"Don't know such a person. Come back later, we're in the middle of an ex-i-bition." It was then that I heard the faint sounds of bones clacking and a steady drumming of feet.

"Is that the police?" someone shouted. "I do not want any more trouble."

"I'll show you who. Calm yourself," she said. "You ain't the police?"

"No."

The door swung open. A woman was standing before me; at least two heads taller than I, with a stiff black mane of weed-dry hair. She put her hands to her lips and motioned me inside. The clacking and drumming grew louder.

"You're missing it, Helen!" a voice rang out over the strange din.

She took my hand, leading me through our old parlor—the bare walls, shredded drapes, and clusters of cats and rabbits that seemed to be everywhere—a ruin of immense proportion.

In the dining room was a stick-thin man in black face tap dancing atop a large, round table. The woman handed me a cooking spoon and an iron skillet.

"Keep time!" she demanded.

The man's white lips curved in a huge smile, his teeth clicked together as he danced. On his head was a Union soldier's kepi. "Says old Abe's come a-courting," he sang. "This time he's won de war, my little gal says—Helen? What does he say?"

"Hallyloo!" she cried and grabbed my spoon, giving the skillet a hearty clang.

"And sashays cross de floor." With that, he did a back flip, ending on his feet, his legs like rubber strings wobbling back and forth.

"Clap at least if you don't have money to throw," the woman called Helen admonished.

I clapped.

"You Willie No Bones," she said. "You give me the itch."

He clawed at himself.

"Lice!"

"Ain't no lice here, you ain't in the hoosegow no more." She turned to me. "He was in the Old Capital for a time."

"I'm sorry?"

"After Johnny Booth killed Abe—bless him forever for what he did," she added, raising the skillet and the spoon. "Do a flip again for the lady." He did a backwards somersault, and landed on the floor in front of my face.

"How-dee-doo!" he crowed.

"When he told the truth," she said, "nobody listened. He was so crazy for so long folks got used to his puppet face that was mistook for a hello, or a scream."

"Like this." He shrieked loud and long.

"Shet it, Will, I'm talking to this lady."

"Is she from Washington City?"

"No, old tiger, she's from right here. Aren't you?"

I winced.

"Here?" he said.

"That is so, sir," I answered. "Nearby, that is. How long have you lived in this, this house?"

"Yanks trashed the place, see," said Helen. "Then they left and we came on in."

"We used to live by Mrs. Mary Surratt's boarding house over on H Street," he said. "Before they stretched her neck, they carted us all off like we were cattle."

"Even dear John Booth's whore," Helen said. "Go on with your testament, No-Bones, so I can have a piss."

"I knew most all the yarns that grew to be lies that I told about the folks down there on H Street," he said, shuffling this way and that. "Some of 'em was true, you see. So when I told that I knew Mrs. Surratt's boy Johnny was up to no good, nobody did believe me. I told the constable that Johnny Surratt was in a band of plotters against Abe Lincoln that left at all hours, snuffing his mama's candle and jeering on the day Richmond fell to the North."

"Did you know John Booth?" I asked.

"Nope. But I know he fired the sun with his smile and did a brave thing."

He saw me wince and patted my hand. "He's long gone now. When they took me away, I said I didn't know beans about him. The constable listened for a minute, but then I told him I saw red all the time.

"There is big bands of red dancing down my arms, on my tongue. There is red lamps in the basement, on all night so I can't ever sleep. The red is fastened to the dream tender who lives upstairs and sucks the nightmares away with a flat, sorry face and a long, red tongue, and the lick tastes of hot candy. I served seventy-two days in the Old Capitol Prison after Old Abe was popped. Never could finger me, but they sure bagged old Dr. Mudd, didn't they? They ain't got the half of us."

"I'll heed that, Mr. No-Bones," I said.

"Pleased to please," he said and did a stumble-down tap dance, ending in a bow to me.

"Ain't he beeeutiful?" crooned Helen. "He used to dance with Callie's Minstrel Show at the Varieties Theatre on Ninth Street near The Avenue."

"At the end of the show I keened like a colored woman who'd lost all her babies," Willie said, falling flat to the floor. "Sometimes the soldiers threw money at me. I could always spot the good coins through the smoke."

"May I have a look around?" I asked.

"Sure," said Helen. "I sleep up in the sister's room now. She's dead, you see. No-Bones here snores and swears the whole night long."

"I got bad dreams, woman!"

"Shet it. Let's take her upstairs." With that she dragged No-Bones to his feet.

The door to my parents' room was closed. I opened it.

Helen slammed it shut. "Hell no, you'll let the rabbits out, if they ain't copulating, that is."

I moved down the hall to my bedroom. Gone now my small chair and table with the vase of violets always fresh. My old bed was sagging and covered with cats. Old yellow Toms and Tabbies were peering at me.

"Now here is the sacred place," No-Bones said, opening the door to my brother's room.

A crucifix lay on the bed. Next to it was a full-sized effigy in a Confederate uniform—a crudely molded young face with a black moustache. John Wilkes Booth had come home.

"God save the South," whispered No-Bones.

"Time for his nap," Helen said, steering me to the stairs.

"Next time you come, bring money," No-Bones said.

"There won't be a next time," I answered.

"Charlotte town is burning down," he sang. "Goodbye, goodbye. Charlotte Town is burning down, goodbye, Liza Jane."

O, let no words but deeds revenge this treason
Henry VI, Part I by William Shakespeare

30

It was past dusk. I returned to the edge of the meadow.

"Are you there, Asia?" It was my husband's voice.

"Yes."

"I can't see you."

"Nor I you, husband."

"Darkness came so quickly," he said.

"I know."

"Are you coming, then?"

"You never talked about the prison, John."

"You never asked."

"Did they harm you?"

"In some ways. Others suffered more."

"I'm sorry."

"Thank you for that."

"I need one more day, please, before we leave for England."

"For what?" he asked.

"Gillian and Hulbert, I want a few hours with them alone. And for our son to say a proper goodbye as well."

"All right."

"Just that?"

"Yes. I understand. All right."

"I can't see you, husband."

"Here is my hand, Asia."

"I have it."

We walked to the carriage. I heard the cries of descending night birds, and little else.

The uncertain glory of an April day, which now shows all the beauty of the sun, and by and by a cloud takes all away.
    The Two Gentlemen of Verona
    by William Shakespeare

Epilogue

Bournemouth, England
April 15, 1867

In rain, the beach is a moonscape, rockbound and endless with gray-tipped black waves. And a half-circle sun smirks like a half-wit in a cloud-banked sky. I do not mind it so. I can walk for many a mile and not see a single face. My son sleeps well in the salt-laced air. I do not mind it so. I am just Mrs. Clarke, now, you see.

Mrs. Clarke is a good neighbor. She is want to bring honey cakes to the ailing old and recites poems to the children of the village when they ask.

Mrs. Clarke is no longer a Booth, as though the name was covered over by sand—formless and very far away. Each day I cull memory and scrape my mind clean of him until he is but a shadow on the English rocks. I will pack all that remains of him deep in my heart, which is less than a heart now. It is an organ that pumps and prods me to life every day, nothing more.

Mr. Clarke is most occupied with his theatre and his actresses. He pays proper attention to his son who brings back all lost laughter, all lost love to me. The boy is bold and beautiful, and is want to recite snippets of verses like he was born to the task.

A letter came from Gillian today. I hold it against my heart before I open it.

My dearest Asia,

Your mama wishes for me to tell you she is surely missing you and the child but says you know your papa cannot find her all the way in England. I said Mr. Junius could fly across any ocean like he had the map in his hand but she would not have it.

Hulbert and me will keep her here with us. She does give our students a tickle when she sings those old songs and throws a bit of Shakespeare their way. They call her "Mrs. Fairy" and treat her so gentle. She is a teacher, you see like she was born to it.

I don't want you to worry for us as we now have ten students, all of them a fair shade of ebony like me save for one boy who was left at the door. He is a white child, and mute as the dead but is learning to read and make words with his mouth. Trouble is, no sound but air comes out but he is a God-sent soul who will be luck for us, that, I know.

Hulbert goes off now and again, looking for folks who are still fixing to find freedom. They have it mostly but need a hawk-man to keep one sharp ear to the wind. Mostly he keeps here. Of that I am glad and the sweet sight of him makes me brighter than the sun. He asks to be remembered to you and the child.

I pray for you, Asia. I will come to you for a short while as soon as I can make the fare for the crossing. Hulbert will keep care of your mama. Right now, she would not keep a lick of health on the sea what with her weak chest and rheumatism.

> My love to the end of my days,
> Gillian James
> Hulbert signs to you below.
> Keep strong. I don't forget you.
> H.J.

Dearest Gillian,

I have decided to write our story, in secret, of course, as Mr. Clarke would surely burn it if he knew. I will send it to you in a plain package for safekeeping. Or better, when you come to me, if you come to me, I shall place it in your hands myself. Please ask Hulbert to stay close.

> My love to you,
> Asia

Author's note

Asia Booth Clarke lived the rest of her life in England. During her self-imposed exile, she wrote the story of her lost brother, John Wilkes, that would be published in 1938 as *The Unlocked Book*. She wrote in secret, of course.

In 1888, she died at the age of fifty-two of heart failure. At her request, her body was brought to America. She rests near her brother in the Green Mount Cemetery in Baltimore, Maryland.

April 9, 1865
Lee Surrenders to Grant at Appomattox. The Civil War is over.

April 14, 1865
John Wilkes Booth shoots Abraham Lincoln at point blank range at Ford's Theatre.

April 15-April 26
Asia Booth Clarke is held under house arrest. Booth remains at large.

April 26, 1865
Booth is cornered in a tobacco barn at Port Royal, Virginia where he is shot and killed.

Acknowledgments

As I tumbled through time with the reckless, enchanted and ill-fated Booth family, I had much guidance, love and support throughout this project; this tale of lives lived in uncommon dissonance, and with fierce love.

To the muses, mentors, and loved ones . . .

My husband Chuck Eckstein, my brother James, Lisa, Raleigh and Miles Singer, Hariet, Missy Eckstein, David Burgess, and Judy Oppenheimer . . . love, always.

And to my daughter Jessica, who willingly shares the endless rabbit holes of history with me, thank you for now, and then, and soon again.

For Stanley Eckstein—for believing . . . Rest well.

To the late, glad-hearted Dr. James O. Hall, "pater familias" of Lincoln assassination research, I promise to keep illuminating the lives and struggles of "the little-known men and women in the great, big wars."

To my family of friends and artists—Larry Masser, Susan Chieco, Michael Nelson, Judith Messinger,

Susanne and Martin Malles, Erik Seastrand, Joanna Rubiner, Margaret Travolta, Becky Bonar, Ken Deifik, Enn Rytell, Steve Hytner, Douglas Rye, Donna Rawlins, Drew Bell, and Ed Cunningham, much love and appreciation.

And to the able scholars, authors and chums— John Stewart, Charles Higham, Robert Scott Davis, John Stanton, David Gaddy, Laurie Verge, Joan Chaconas, Edward Steers, Jr., Michael and Marjorie Kauffman, and Terry Alford, may we continue to pry the past from its rusty hinges.

For Sandra Fallon, an "earth angel." Thanks beyond thanks. To Deborah Smith, and the shining women of Belle Books/Bell Bridge, I'm glad beyond measure that my work came to rest in your able keep.

Center Point Publishing
600 Brooks Road ● PO Box 1
Thorndike ME 04986-0001 USA

(207) 568-3717

US & Canada:
1 800 929-9108
www.centerpointlargeprint.com